THE UNFORGETTING

A PSYCHOLOGICAL THRILLER

BONNIE TRAYMORE

The Unforgetting: A Psychological Thriller
Copyright © 2025 Bonnie Traymore
All Rights Reserved

This is a work of fiction. Names, places, characters, and incidents are either the product of the author's imagination or are used fictitiously, and any resemblance to actual persons, living or dead, businesses, organizations, events, or locales is entirely coincidental.

No part of this book may be reproduced or transmitted in any form or by any means, electronic or mechanical, including photocopying, recording, or by any information storage and retrieval system, without permission in writing from the author.

First Edition
Honolulu, Hawai'i
Pathways Publishing
Paperback ISBN 979-8-218-57528-1

ALSO BY BONNIE TRAYMORE

Killer Motives

Little Loose Ends

The Stepfamily

The Guest House

Head Case

The Bluff

A Little Getaway

For my family

"It's no use going back to yesterday, because I was a different person then."

-Alice's Adventures in Wonderland

PROLOGUE
TEN YEARS EARLIER

The crackling flames feel close.
Too close.
The heat licks my face.
"She's gonna fall in," I hear someone say.
Not me.
They can't be talking about me.
Because I'm floating.
Floating people can't fall.
Gyrating to the rhythm of the blaring music, I want to be one with the flames. They dance in a way I envy, shooting up and down in sharp angles, casting shadows over the partiers, giving them a ghoulish look. Some of the people I know. Many I don't. We twist and writhe and merge with the music.
Nirvana.
So fitting.
The smell of burning wood permeates my nostrils, mixing with reefer and patchouli oil. Embers float down like

sparkling rubies in the twinkling night sky. A red-hot one lands on my shoulder. I bat it off, singeing the hairs on my hand, but I don't flinch.

This is what the afterlife must feel like. When you become a bodiless bundle of energy, no longer tethered to the corporal world, free to roam around the atmosphere.

A blood-curdling scream comes from...somewhere.

Something bad is happening.

But we don't stop.

We can't stop.

We keep dancing and laughing and soon the flames are too hot and it's not fun anymore and I think maybe, just maybe, that was my scream I heard in the woods.

NOW

ONE

REAGAN

"Please, just leave him for a little while, Mom. He'll settle down."

My mother rolls her eyes.

It's going to be one of those days.

I want her help. I need her help. And I resent the fact that I need her help. It's always been like that with us. Maybe it's like that with all mothers and daughters. If she'd only take it down a notch, perhaps we'd find our groove. I'm thirty-one, though, so I don't hold out much hope. Radical acceptance, my therapist tells me.

Accept what you can't change.

Change what you can.

So, I take a deep breath and try to appreciate the fact that my mother's willing to drop everything and come to my rescue, and I don't push back when she ignores me and lifts my squalling four-month-old infant out of his bouncy seat and walks him around our living room for the millionth time. She started this, and now he expects it all the time.

They say I've got postpartum depression, but I think that's just another label society slaps on people like me, trying to fit us into a neat little box with a clear set of instructions about how to fix us and get us back on track.

The patronizing bothers me the most.

We're here for you, Reagan.

You're strong.

You can do it.

But what if I can't?

MY HUSBAND COMES HOME, eager to snatch the baby from my arms. He used to kiss me hello, but that seems to have gone by the wayside. Matt's a great guy. Everyone tells me that. But they say it in a way that implies I should be grateful.

He's a catch, Reagan.

Subtext?

Don't screw this up.

"Where's your mother?" Matt asks.

"She went to the store," I reply, trying not to read too much into his wary intonation. Trying not to feel like he was worried that I was home alone with our baby.

He hands me a stack of mail and finally gives me a peck on the lips. "Can you sort this?" he asks.

We used to be a hot couple, before I turned into a baby vessel and a milk machine. I miss our old life. I miss us. And I feel guilty about that. I had one session with a postpartum specialist, and she says my feelings are common and totally understandable, which is good to know. But it doesn't fix the problem, does it?

I look through the stack of mail while Matt cuddles baby Danny.

A hospital bill.

A credit card offer.

An envelope postmarked Saratoga Springs, New York, addressed to Reagan Hansen.

It looks like some kind of invitation.

My stomach clenches, a strange mixture of dread and excitement zapping some life into me. It's been ten years since I graduated from college. Ten years since the night that derailed my life and plunged me into a very dark place. Before I even open the envelope, I have a sinking feeling that I know what it is. Tossing it in the trash would be the right thing to do. I know this. But of course, I don't.

I rip it open.

A surge of energy courses through me.

It's an invitation.

For a weekend gathering.

At Ella's family camp.

Everyone's been telling me to take some time for myself. And I think it's about time I listen to them. Is this insane? Dropping everything and leaving my family to return to the place that landed me in a very troubled state of mind?

But I have to go. I have a pressing need to go. Because I know that somewhere in my memory of that night is the key to unlocking what's eating at me. Something I need to face, so I can heal and fully move on.

"YOU WANT TO DO WHAT?" My mother's raised eyebrows question my sanity as she gathers her things to leave for the day.

I tell her about the reunion, or rather, the gathering of healing and reflection, as it's being dubbed. "Ella's organizing it. You said I should get away. Take some time for myself."

A look of concern washes over her face, but then she forces a smile. "That's true," Mom says. "I did say that. Sure, honey, I can help over the weekend. You know I can't get enough of this little guy. And it might be nice for you to see Ella again."

She reaches down and tickles Danny, who's cradled in my arms.

I catch her eye and offer her a smile.

I know she's worried about me, and the idea of my going back to the camp. And I can't say I blame her after what happened ten years ago, along with my recent setback. The look on her face before she forced the smile conveyed her message clearly.

Are you sure?

Be careful.

But she caught herself before she voiced her concerns, which means she's starting to trust me more. Because how can I learn to trust myself, if the people around me fill me with self-doubt? This makes me feel heard. She's trying. And not everyone is so lucky to have a mom like her who is there for me and her grandson, whenever we need her—and sometimes when we don't. I really should show her more appreciation.

As she's leaving, I call out to her. "Mom?" I say.

"Yes, Reagan?"

"I love you," I say. "And thanks. For everything."

My mom stops and smiles, and that makes my heart melt a little.

"I love you, too, sweetheart," she says. "And you're welcome."

ELLA PARKER IS the only person I've kept in touch with from that period in my life, although we're pretty much down to social media posts and yearly Christmas cards. I suppose it's Ella Williams now, but she'll always be Ella Parker to me. We were closer once. Not best friend close, but closer than we are now.

That was a long time ago, though. Before everything changed. Ella's always had the upper hand in the friendship, and that might be one of the reasons I've distanced myself from her. I've always been a bit intimidated by her, and that's not a great basis for a healthy friendship. My insecurities had consequences, too. Big ones.

Her parents own a family camp near Lake Placid, New York, in the High Peaks region of the Adirondack Mountains, a collection of forty-six peaks in the northernmost part of the range. Calling it a camp is a stretch, since it's basically a large cabin plus a few storage buildings, but that's what they call it. Wealthy city dwellers started building these "Great Camps" in the Adirondacks during the Gilded Age, when they needed a respite from the rat race, some of the bigger ones now serving as inns or tourist attractions. During our college years at an upstate university a few hours away, a group of us would meet there, at her camp, at the close of the school year for a weekend-long celebration.

Her family's rustic cabin provided the basics: a toilet, a shower, a well-equipped kitchen facility. They also own about ten acres of wilderness surrounding the structure. Some of us would spread out on the mountain and camp out under the stars, some would sleep in the cabin. All six of us in our little gang, plus the locals she knew who sometimes joined in for the partying but never stayed over. Ecstasy-infused mini-ragers interspersed with deep, philosophical musings around the fire pit about the meaning of life.

Random hook-ups.

Fractious friendships.

One lasting marriage.

And one tragic death.

Ella's couching this as a memorial for Lanie Martin. A gathering of remembrance, healing, and reflection, she's calling it. A chance to come together and pay tribute to a life cut way too short.

It's not being billed as a weekend of partying, trying to recreate the good old days, ala *The Big Chill*. It's supposed to be a time for reflection and healing, which is likely the reason she's not calling it a college reunion, although that's pretty much what it is. A ten-year reunion, at Ella's camp. But rather than marking the anniversary of a joyous occasion —our college graduation and a new beginning in life—it's forever marking the tragic death of our friend at the very same location ten years ago.

We'd promised, in those alcohol-infused days, that the six of us would meet at the camp every year, no matter where life took us, for one weekend of bonding and abandon. After

Lanie's accident, that plan went by the wayside. Sobered us right up. We never spoke of reunions at the camp again.

But here's the thing. I'm not sure that Lanie's death was an accident. The working theory is that she walked into the woods to pee, drunk, and stumbled off the mountainside and down into a ravine, snapping her neck in the fall.

Which is possible.

Sure.

But I saw something that night, and I didn't tell the police about it, at Ella's insistence. For that, I feel guilty, and my bad decision still haunts me. Then there are the nightmares, and this strange feeling in my gut that I know more than I can recall. Visions and snippets of memory that sometimes visit me in my dreams and are now invading my conscious mind.

I was wasted that night, I'm sorry to say, and because of that, I'm not sure if it's the power of suggestion or the guilt causing these vague flashes, or if something traumatic happened and I've blocked it out.

All this time, I thought the dreams were a result of my drug and alcohol-induced state, or some kind of PTSD aftermath. The faint memories that sometimes crossed into my conscious mind, I figured for hallucinations. But in my postpartum state, I've been starting to remember things. Little flashes here and there that seem more authentic. These memories are clearer. More fully formed. Something important is hovering on the edge of my consciousness; I can feel it.

Perhaps it should stay there.

But I have a feeling it could be the key to straightening my head out. To being able to take care of my baby and stay married to Matt the Great Guy and finally get everyone to lay off of me.

Because I think something happened to Lanie that night.

And it's possible that I know more than I think I do.

Is it a bad idea?

A potentially dangerous idea?

Like in a horror movie when the star hears a noise in the basement and goes down to check instead of calling the police?

Yes. Just like that. It's a very bad idea.

But just like the lead in a horror movie, I can't help myself.

I'm heading down the stairs.

TWO
REAGAN

My mother has left for the day and it's just me and Matt now. We've finished dinner; Danny's asleep in his portable crib, near the TV. Just the two of us, but it doesn't feel like it. The weighty responsibility of parenthood hangs in the air like a thick cloud of smoke. I constantly feel as if my throat is about to close up, with all that can go wrong.

I've struggled with anxiety all my life. It got worse after Lanie's death, but nothing like it is now, with a precious, helpless infant under my care. People think I'm eager to pass him off to others because I've somehow failed to bond with him.

But that's not it. It's that I don't trust myself. I'm afraid I'll drop him on his head or hold him wrong or forget to take the blanket away or smother him when we both fall dead asleep while he's in my arms. You're not supposed to do that, but it happens when you're so sleep-deprived you don't even know what day it is anymore. People don't tell you the truth about having a baby. It's terrifying and tiring and never-ending.

There are moments of pure joy, it's true. At four months, Danny can smile now, and when he gives me that Duchenne grin, the kind that reaches the eyes, oxytocin shoots through my veins like a shot of morphine. But I can't seem to make it happen. It's random, as if he's simply testing out a new skill, not really smiling at me in particular.

Matt places a hand on my shoulder as he plops next to me on the milk-stained sofa. "How are you doing today, honey?" he asks.

His patronizing tone bothers me. He's treating me like a mental patient rather than his lover. "Fine," I say, fearing it's going to be a while before I can live this down.

It was one weak moment.

I wish they would all just let it go.

We've made love a few times since the birth, but he handles me with kid gloves. This makes me feel fragile and powerless, but I don't know how to tell him that. He's trying to be gentle. I should appreciate it. Nothing he does feels right, and I'm constantly on his case. The specialist tells me it's the hormones. It will pass, she assures me.

But what if it doesn't?

If he would only grab me. Kiss me. Look at me with hungry passion in his eyes, the kind of passion that started us down this path to parenthood, I think it would all be okay. I should tell him this.

But I don't.

"Matt?" I say.

"Yes?"

"There's this reunion in a few weeks." I proceed to tell

him about it. A weekend getaway, about two hours from where we live—a generic upscale suburb of Albany, New York.

He nods along as I explain what it's for.

A memorial for Lanie Martin.

He knows most of what happened that weekend. And, out of anyone, he knows how profoundly it affected me. It almost broke us up.

Matt was the one who saved me from myself and dealt with the aftermath. But I haven't shared much detail about my resurfacing memories, partly because I don't want to call attention to my state of inebriation that weekend, although he knows that Lanie's death has been on my mind a lot these days. I was intentionally vague when I mentioned my spotty snips of memory and my dreams, and I didn't let on that I have doubts that her death was an accident.

I haven't told anyone about the feeling in my gut that something more happened, not even my therapist. Not yet, because I'm not sure I even want to know, or if it would be in my best interest to tell anyone until I have more information. It's possible I'll only incriminate myself, especially since I failed to tell the cops what I saw.

Tell me not to go.

"It's up to you," he says. "Maybe it will be good for you. Lanie's been on your mind lately. Maybe this will help give you some closure. Your mom can help me with Danny."

It'll be good for him, is what he means.

Matt needs space, I can tell.

And I can't say I blame him. I've been hard to deal with lately. But he doesn't understand how hard it is. The hormone swings. The sore breasts. The body that looks like it belongs to another person. I've been having a hard time breastfeeding, and we've finally given in and switched to formula. For that, I feel like a colossal failure.

"In the interest of full disclosure, I called Ella a few weeks back," he says. "To let her know you were having a hard time with everything."

My eyes widen. "Matt? Why would you do that?"

He offers an explanation. "Because she went through the same trauma, and I thought it would be good for you to reconnect with her. And then she floated the idea of a gathering. That was the last I heard of it."

"Any more secrets you want to disclose?" I ask.

He lets out a sigh. "Reagan. Don't be like that. It'll be good for you. I promise."

"Fine," I say, crossing my arms in front of me. "I don't want to talk about it anymore."

Matt points the remote at the TV, opens the Netflix app, and shoots me a sideways glance, taking in my viewing habits.

"What's with you and the true crime lately?" he asks.

I shrug. "I like it. It relaxes me. Gets my mind off my problems."

"You're a curious one." He pulls me in and kisses me on the top of my head. Then he lands on something. A new thriller mini-series that should keep us occupied for a while.

"Good?" he asks.

"Sure," I say. "But I'm fine with a rom-com."

"No. Too predictable," he says. "And too sappy."

"But what's the difference between a thriller and true crime? I mean, people still die."

"Not real people," he says.

He puts his arm around me, and we settle in for a few hours of mindless TV, which is about as intimate as it gets these days.

THAT WAS A SURPRISE.

When we got upstairs and placed our sleeping infant in his crib in the next room, I plopped down in bed and prepared to drift off. But then Matt reached over and touched my arm, and something shifted. It was spontaneous and natural, unlike our previous post-birth encounters, which felt scripted and stiff. I have no idea what prompted it on his end. Maybe it was the thought of my leaving for a few days.

Our lovemaking was tender and steamy, loving and genuine. And as I lie in bed listening to the rhythm of my husband's breathing as he drifts off, I feel hopeful about the future for the first time since Danny was born.

I'm not tired, though, and my mind drifts back to the evening of Lanie's death. For the longest time, all I could remember was being by the raging fire.

Oppressive heat.

A blood-curdling scream.

I seem to have passed out, or that's what Ella told me. Sort of fell into the fire pit, which that year turned into more of a raging bonfire, fueled by a bunch of townies who'd crashed the party. But I was informed that someone grabbed me and pulled me back before I did too much damage.

In those days, ecstasy was the wonder drug. Nothing bad could happen on it, or so we thought. The six of us were inseparable in our college days. Lanie, Ella, and me and our three guy friends: Ted, Josh, and Brady, who we called Brainy. He was premed, and the most serious student of the six of us. The first year, it was just the six of us up at the camp.

But over the years, some of Ella's local friends joined in. That last year, there must have been forty of them, or more. Some she knew. Some she didn't. And that's when things started to get weird. It was a rough crowd. Most of them older than us. Stoners. Bikers. A few aging hippy types mixed in.

One of the bikers, a burly guy with stringy blond hair and a tattoo on his forearm, tried to grab me and kiss me. I rejected him, and he set his sights on Lanie. We looked a little alike. Same type. Both of us had long, dark hair, but hers had more of a reddish undertone that wouldn't have been visible at night. Maybe he thought of us as interchangeable.

And I drank.

A lot.

When I'm uncomfortable, that's what I do. Combined with Zoloft and the molly, well, do the math on that one. Needless to say, my memory of that night is a little spotty. But one thing I'm starting to remember is Lanie and someone arguing after I fell in the fire.

Or was it earlier?

And I swear I saw someone grab Lanie by the shoulder and whip her around toward them.

Was it the biker guy?

I have no idea.

In my memory and in my dream, he doesn't have a face.

It could have been a dream. Or a hallucination. It could have happened before I heard the scream.

Or maybe it didn't happen at all.

We didn't even know about her fall until the morning, when we couldn't find her. I told my friends about the scream I heard coming from the woods. Nobody else seemed to have heard it. People were shouting and laughing, so it could have been a different kind of scream. Perhaps I'd misinterpreted it, as Ella suggested.

When we realized she was missing, we scoured the woods surrounding the cabin and spotted Lanie at the bottom of the ravine, her body twisted and lifeless. It felt surreal to me, I remember that much. Like it wasn't really happening. I thought maybe it was the drug hangover, or that perhaps there was something wrong with me because I wasn't feeling anything.

Later, my therapist suggested I'd been in shock, which I figured, even before I started seeing her. I went from having no feelings to having them consume me.

Grief. Loss. Confusion.

And guilt.

Especially the guilt.

Because everyone flipped into self-preservation mode. The fact that our friend was lying dead in a ravine became secondary to our panic about how this would affect us.

If we called the cops, would we get busted?

Were the drugs still in our system?

Even me, with my suspicions about what happened to her, the scream I may have heard, and the biker guy who accosted me and Lanie, I was more worried about myself. I feel terrible about that. Ella was the most distraught, because she thought she'd get in trouble with her parents, or that they might get sued. We delayed the emergency call so we could get rid of the damning evidence. Everyone seemed eager to chalk it up to a tragic accident, even after I mentioned that I'd seen the biker guy chatting Lanie up.

Ella barked at me, "No bikers were here, Reagan! Got it?"

I got it, that's for sure.

I kept my mouth shut about the biker guy, even when the cops asked if I'd seen anything unusual. Another thing I feel horrible about.

What if he killed my friend and got away with it?

Ella was eager to close that chapter of our lives.

We rarely spoke of it again.

We graduated soon after.

Drifted apart.

And now she wants to have a memorial weekend for Lanie Martin.

Interesting.

THREE
REAGAN

It's Saturday, the morning after our passionate evening. Matt's off today, so it's the three of us, which gives my mother a much-needed break, even if she acts like she doesn't need one. I can tell that Danny stresses her out sometimes, but she'll never admit that to me. She wants to be strong, but sometimes I wish she would let her guard down a little.

It makes me feel inadequate, the way she swoops in and tries to solve all my problems before I even know they exist. I'll never live up to her example, so perhaps that's why I don't try very hard. She's always telling me how she wants to be everything her mother wasn't—grandmother, she claims, was a self-centered alcoholic who didn't give a damn about her—but there's such a thing as overcompensation.

"Hey," I say as my husband stumbles into the kitchen in a fog.

"It smells great in here. What are you baking?"

"Pumpkin scones," I say.

There's a batch on the cooling rack, a batch in the oven,

and enough batter for another, which is way more than we can eat. I usually bring some over to the elderly couple next door, which they appreciate. They've been good to us, even staying with the baby one night about a month ago, until my mother could get here.

The night of my incident.

But I don't want to think about that now.

Matt reaches for one but I bat his hand away.

"They're too hot. Be patient," I say.

"Ooh, but they smell so good," he says. Then he shrugs and makes himself a cup of coffee.

I let Matt sleep in this morning. I'm getting more confident with Danny as the months wear on. Matt kisses me softly on the lips.

"Thanks for letting me sleep in. I slept so hard, I feel like I'm drunk or something. In a good way." He smiles. "And thanks for the scones."

I smile back.

Baking is a hobby of mine. Or more like therapy, if I'm being honest. I've always loved to bake, for as long as I can remember. It's something my mother taught me, and I have fond memories of us in the kitchen sifting and mixing and frosting birthday cakes. She was a great mom like that, as far as handing me down traditions. She tried other ones like knitting and needlepoint, but baking is the only one that stuck. The buttery smell in the air reminds me of childhood and innocence, and I hope that Danny's taking it all in, forming some lovely memories for himself.

But that's not the only reason I like to bake—the fond memories with my mother. Baking is a precision sport. It's not like cooking, where you can experiment and use a pinch of this or a shake of that, freestyling it rather than following the recipe. Baking is a science, and if the wrong amount of baking powder or salt or oil is used, it will ruin the entire process. The clarity is what appeals to me. There's no decision-making involved. Just follow the recipe to a tee and *voila!* You've nailed it.

Life is rarely, if ever, like that, especially for me. I'm not great with decisions, and I'm constantly doubting myself. Analysis paralysis is a term I feel was invented just for me. Take picking a major in college. I was "undeclared" for the first year, until Lanie convinced me to try marketing, because there were a lot of cute guys in her classes. We had fun making up stories about them as we admired them from afar instead of paying attention to the professor; at least until we both almost failed our midterm. And house hunting? Even though there wasn't a lot on the market, I finally had to tell Matt to surprise me. Who does that? But it was nearly killing me, trying to decide between the three we'd narrowed it down to.

And so, I bake.

Matt's happy that I'm back at it, I can tell, and not just because he's got a sweet tooth. This is the first time I've baked anything since Danny was born; unless you count Sunday morning pancakes, which in all fairness, should probably not count. He knows that this is a good sign. I'm coming back from the darkness.

My husband looks cute this morning, with his thick dark hair all rumpled and a light stubble dusting his square jaw. It feels nice to do something for him for a change.

"What do you want to do today?" I ask.

His eyes widen. They are deep brown with flecks of

gold, which I can see this morning because he's not wearing his glasses. "You feel like doing something?"

I try not to let it bother me that he seems shocked by this notion and just be happy about the fact that the dark cloud of depression is finally starting to lift.

"Sure," I say. "Why not? I'm going out of town in two weeks. Let's have a family day."

We bat around some ideas.

The zoo. Mini golf. A stroll around the mall.

But we don't land on anything.

"I'm going to take a shower," I say. "I'll think about it."

Our home is larger than it needs to be for two people and a baby, and nicer than we deserve at our age, although this isn't, generally speaking, an overly expensive area. A four-bedroom, two-and-a-half-bath Craftsman on a one-acre lot with a chef's kitchen, a gas fireplace, and a two-car garage—on a cul-de-sac. Almost cliché. I can't complain. From the outside, my life looks perfect. Inside my head, it's another story. I wonder if it's like that for most people, or if I'm somehow different.

Matt makes good money. He's got an MBA and he's a vice president at an insurance company. A good, stable job, which allows me to stay home with Danny. We say we want another child soon, and I can only hope the next one doesn't bash me over the head as much as this one did. I've been working part-time from home a little, at least I was until the incident. Now everyone wants me to take it easy, which isn't helping me at all.

Truthfully, I don't get much satisfaction out of my marketing job, and I'd love to do something more meaningful. But I fear if I say that out loud to Matt or my mother, they'll call me flaky or unfocused. Working from home isn't all it's cracked up to be, either. I like getting out of the house. And as much as I've been reluctant to go out and do things, staying home depresses me. It's a vicious cycle, you see. And I'm the only one who can break it.

I'd like to say there's a good reason I've struggled so much over the years to stay on the right path. Like I had horrible parents or someone died when I was young or we lived through a horrifying natural disaster or I was kidnapped by a madman and have terrifying PTSD episodes. But the truth is, I'm just wired that way.

My parents are divorced, so there's that. But lots of people have divorced parents. They both love me. We all get along. My father lives in Seattle now so I don't see him as much as I did before. But they stayed together until I left for college. My younger brother was more affected than I was. Truthfully, I have no good excuse for the stress I put them through.

Aside from my brain chemistry, that is, which my new therapist says is not my fault. Maybe I can start to believe her. She seems better than the others, but I don't want to get my hopes up.

You're your own worst enemy, Reagan.

I've heard that phrase from more than one person over the years, as if anyone would choose to be their own worst enemy. Obviously, I can't help it. I'm not purposefully tanking my own life.

In middle school, an eating disorder surfaced. Later, I had some run-ins with drug and alcohol abuse. Faulty wiring, my new therapist says. She's trying to reprogram me with DBT—a kind of behavioral therapy—and a new

SSRI, which I swear doesn't help, but I've agreed to give it a go.

My anxiety has caused me to do stupid things over the years. Drink too much. Do drugs, especially in my early college years.

Almost blow it with Matt.

One therapist suggested I intentionally tanked my relationship with Matt because deep inside, I never felt I deserved him. Some kind of twisted self-loathing, she claimed. I'm not sure that's true. I think I just wasn't ready for a guy like him. Lots of young women are like that. Isn't that the trope of the teen romance story? Liking the bad boy who's so deliciously wrong? It's only after you've been burned by a few of them that you learn. I love Matt. I appreciate him now.

You need to learn to love yourself first, Reagan.

That was the kind of psychobabble that got crammed down my throat over the years. It's pretty much the stupidest thing a therapist ever said to me, and I'm trying not to let that color my opinion of the one I have now.

I wasn't *that* bad, after all. It's not like I killed someone. I wasn't a mean girl in school. I graduated from high school and college on time. Generally speaking, it's been two steps forward and one step back. But I did give my parents a fair bit of grief, and I've had two major setbacks.

One was right after graduation, after Lanie died.

The other was a month or so after Danny's birth.

Could there be a connection between those two events?

I started thinking about Lanie's death a lot once Danny was born, and the memory of that night seemed to be connected somehow to my worsening depression. At first, I thought it was guilt. I lived—to have a husband and a family and a life. Lanie didn't.

But I feel like it's more than that. Like there's some other connection I can't see yet. So, my therapist and I have been working on techniques to try to help me remember. To see if there's something I'm perhaps blocking out. Something traumatic that had to do with her death, or if my spotty memory is simply due to the drugs and alcohol I imbibed that weekend. Of course, it could be a little of both.

That evening, I took ecstasy on top of booze and an SSRI, and my therapist tells me that it's possible that some of my memories from that evening will never return, although they still could. I do remember quite a bit from that night, so she's hopeful I might regain some of the lost ones. The evening sits in my mind in chunks, some of them out of order, from what the others have told me. It's not like I lost the whole night.

For this reason, the therapist calls it a brownout, rather than a blackout. And she said that sometimes, little bits of memory can come back if there's a trigger like a smell or a sound or the sight of something that brings me back into the moment.

A part of me knows I'm playing with fire, heading back to Ella's camp. But another part of me can't resist. Something is hovering on the edge of my consciousness. Maybe I saw or heard or experienced something traumatic, or maybe I heard or saw something during my brownout. Something critical to figuring out what really happened to Lanie and getting me closure—and justice for my friend, if it's not too late for that.

And even if it's something terrible, I owe it to myself and to Lanie to find out what it is.

FOUR
REAGAN

We landed on mini golf, and I'm not sure it was the most practical idea, but we're having fun. We've been inconveniencing the couple behind us, though, because I periodically have to stop if Danny needs a feeding or a diaper change. There's nine holes and we're headed now to number seven.

Danny's piercing cry turns some heads in my direction. I'm walking from the sixth to the seventh hole while pushing the stroller with one hand, with Danny in my arm and the bottle crammed in his mouth. Matt's at the start of the seventh hole, trying to keep us moving. We're both equally terrible at this, and we're not keeping score.

As I approach, I notice that it's a freaky-looking one.

A clown with its mouth wide open, looking almost like a gargoyle.

Are we supposed to try and hit the ball through its open mouth? I mean, that's kind of impossible, and the ball can easily slip around the sides. I don't like clowns generally, and this one is especially creepy.

"Let's take a break," I say. "I need to sit and feed him."

My husband nods. "Sorry. Go ahead of us," he says to the people waiting behind us.

We find a bench, take a seat, and decide to call it a day as far as the golf game is concerned. But it's a beautiful day and the leaves are just starting to turn, so after Danny finishes his feeding, the three of us stroll around the grounds a bit more and enjoy the day. It's nice to be out of the house, getting some fresh air.

Matt reaches over, brushes the hair back from my face, and gives me a peck on the lips. "This is nice," he says. "I can't remember the last time I played mini golf."

"Me either," I reply.

But that's not completely true. The last time I played mini golf was the second semester of sophomore year in college with my party buddies. We made it into a drinking game, and all of us except Brady were wasted by the end of it. Something about drinking out of the flask every time we lost a hole, and I only remember parts of it.

Brady drove us back to our dorm, and he assured us he was fine to drive. But none of us were in a position to judge that. And cramming six people into his aging Corolla was risky. I sat on Josh's lap in the back seat. I remember that much. We were an item that year. Before he dumped me for Lanie, up at Ella's camp at the end of the school year.

Matt doesn't know how bad it got with the partying, although I suspect he has an inkling, and I never gave much detail to him about my little fling with Josh. If I'm being honest, it wasn't a little fling to me. He broke my heart, and I wonder how it will feel seeing him again, or if he'll even show.

Josh did a number on my self-esteem, that's for sure. He's the kind of guy you notice right away when you walk into a bar. Charismatic, flirty, great with women. Kind of like Ted Bundy. He's not a serial killer, I'm pretty sure. But he killed my self-confidence. I fell hard for him, and he dumped me. Up at the camp, actually. At the end of sophomore year. I should be grateful. I ended up with Matt, who treats me like gold. And I'd like to say that was an easy decision. A no-brainer. But really, for a year or so after I started dating Matt, the Josh break-up still stung, probably because he was part of our group, and I had to see him all the time.

This will be different, I tell myself. I'm a married woman with a wonderful husband and a darling baby boy. Josh is single, floundering from job to job, from what I've heard. If living well is the best revenge, I've gotten mine.

So why does it put my stomach in knots to think about seeing him again?

"SO," Matt says as he pulls into the driveway. "Are you looking forward to seeing the gang again?"

I shrug. "I guess. I mean, it's not a very happy occasion, is it? I wonder why Ella decided to organize a reunion, after all this time."

"It's been ten years. Maybe that's why," Matt says, as he fiddles with the car seat. We're back home now, and he's trying to lift the carrier out of its base without waking Danny, who has drifted off.

I correct him. "It's actually a little more than ten years."

"Such a stickler for details," he says.

"I need to go," I say. "I mean, I want to go. To get closure. Everything happened so fast. And then..."

"And then," he says. "Yeah, I get it. It'll be good for you."

Martha, my neighbor, waves at me and calls out to us. "Great to see you out and about, Reagan. Thanks again for the scrumptious muffins."

They're scones, not muffins.

And what does she mean that she's happy to see me out and about?

Matt told me he didn't disclose to her what really happened that night, and I don't want to start an argument, so I let it go.

"You're welcome," I say.

But when we get inside, I change my mind.

"What did Martha mean?"

"Huh? Oh, she meant scones, honey. Not muffins. The ones you made this morning."

I roll my eyes. "I know that, Matt. What did she mean about being happy to see me *out and about*? Did you tell her what really happened?"

Matt sighs but doesn't answer me as he places the baby holder with our sleeping son on the living room floor. Then he turns to me.

"Look, Reagan," he says. "I'm a person too. I needed support. What you did was, well, it took a toll. She caught me at a weak moment. And yeah, I told her what happened. Lots of women get postpartum depression. It's nothing to be ashamed of."

I am ashamed, though.

And angry.

And upset with him.

"You're supposed to have my back, Matt. Not go behind it."

"I have your back, Reagan, more than you know."

"What's that supposed to mean?"

"Nothing," he says.

And I let it go. He's done a lot for me. More than I've done for him. On some level, I can't blame him for needing support.

But I do wonder.

Who else did he tell?

FIVE
ELLA

Ella opens her laptop to check her email, still very unsure about her decision to host a weekend up at her family's camp, and aware of the fact that she can still back out of it. Her husband, Ted, had initially rejected the idea. But he came around, because he realized that it would give them a chance to kill two birds with one stone.

Being from the kind of family that thumbs its nose at evites, Ella opted for printed snail mail invitations for the gathering. A little formal, but then this is a somber occasion, and she felt she owed Lanie that much. But given the tight turnaround, she asked the invitees to email in their RSVPs. She holds her breath as she prepares to check her email. The invitations have surely arrived by now.

Yes, from Reagan.

No response yet from Josh or Brady.

Ella still has an out. If the others can't make it on such short notice, perhaps she'll ask Matt and Reagan to come for a couple's weekend—or maybe she'll dispense with the idea entirely and leave it alone. It was a spontaneous suggestion, borne of a momentary wave of panic, but she grew to rather like the idea. But as she's picturing the five of them back up at the camp in her mind's eye, she feels her chest tighten.

Matt called Ella about a month ago, informing her that Reagan had been experiencing postpartum depression and asking her if Reagan had reached out. Reagan had been thinking a lot about Lanie and her death, he said, ever since Reagan gave birth to their first child. The anniversary of Lanie's death was on the horizon. Perhaps it was affecting her, Matt suggested. Matt also mentioned that Reagan was starting to remember little flashes from that night, and Matt was worried that one of those memories would be a problem for him.

This sent Ella into a tailspin, the idea of Reagan and her memories returning. Reagan had been out-of-her-head drunk that night, and since nothing had surfaced in the past decade, Ella figured they were in the clear as far as Reagan was concerned.

Why would Reagan be remembering things now?
Ten years later?

One explanation occurred to her, and it made her very nervous.

"Have you two been in touch recently?" Matt asked. "And did you ever say anything to her about...you know?"

"No!" Ella assured Matt, in no uncertain terms. "I told you, that had nothing to do with me. That's between you and Reagan. Why would I say anything about it to her? We haven't spoken in years. But what do you mean, she's remembering little flashes? What kind of little flashes?"

Ella's stomach lurched. Because if Reagan was to

remember what Ella feared she could recall, well then, Ella needed to manage the situation very carefully. Ella figured she'd invite Reagan for a weekend at the camp, and if the memory didn't come back to her there, then it wouldn't likely come back at all. And at least if she remembered something while they were together, Ella could explain the situation to Reagan and hopefully get her to see it was in her best interest to keep her mouth shut about it.

So Ella got this half-baked idea, which she blurted out to Matt, to have a ten-year reunion at her camp. Well, not a reunion. More like a commemoration. She was picturing a small memorial service inside a weekend of reconnecting. And later, she and Ted figured that if everyone came, it would give them an opportunity to take care of another loose end from ten years ago.

At first, Matt protested, concerned that if Reagan remembered more from that night, it could make the situation worse.

"Perhaps it would help Reagan heal," Ella offered. "Help all of us, really, to process our grief. It was traumatic. For her, as you know. But also for the rest of us."

It took a bit of convincing, but Matt came around.

And when Ella suggested he come too, he reluctantly declined.

"Someone has to stay with the baby, and Reagan could use a break," Matt said.

Ella found that odd, so she prodded Matt a little. "Are you sure you're not the one who needs a break, Matt? I'm sure it can't be easy, living with Reagan and all of her... issues."

That seemed to irritate Matt. "Reagan and I are fine, Ella," he said flatly.

End of story.

Then he wrapped up their call.

Ella left it at that. It wasn't her finest moment, giving Matt that little dig, but she couldn't resist. It seemed odd to her that he'd want his wife to come here without him when he knew full well that Josh Tanner would probably be here, too, and that Josh and Reagan had history. But that's not her problem or her concern. She couldn't care less about Reagan and Matt's problems.

Well, maybe she could care a little less. She's not above a good piece of gossip. Or at least, that's how she used to be. But Ella doesn't have time for such trivial matters now. That's a luxury she can't afford.

When she attends the PTA meetings or the wine and cheese gatherings or the book fairs or the art openings with the other wealthy suburban socialites, she plays along. Joins in the small talk and the smack talk about who drank too much at the last function or whose husband has been keeping late hours and has wandering eyes, and she wishes for problems like those to be her biggest ones.

Because Ella is still doing damage control from that night ten years ago, and if she lives to be a hundred years old, she's come to terms with the fact that she might never be fully at peace. Secrets are dangerous, and they never die. They live on, as long as the people who harbor them.

And sometimes even longer than that.

SIX
REAGAN

Pulling my car up toward the cabin, I have a sinking feeling in my stomach. Ella's camp sits about a thousand feet up one of the forty-six peaks of the High Peaks region. Around number twenty, I think, maybe four thousand feet high at its summit.

A long, winding, tree-lined dirt road leads to the cabin from the main road, but their ownership starts well before that. The trees form a tunnel, enveloping me and blocking out the sun as my Camry meanders up the mountain. Grasping at my chest, I suddenly feel a little claustrophobic, thinking about how there's only one way up and down, the clunking of rocks under the carriage signifying to me that I need to take it slow, even in good weather.

It's late summer and it's dry today, but rain storms can make the road impassible. There's a hurricane coming up the coast, but we're pretty far inland so we should be fine. It must be treacherous in the winter, though. I probably would not have risked it at a different time of year.

Finally, I arrive at the plateau where her cabin sits, as if it's always been there, hewn out of the mountain itself. Tall maple and birch trees frame it on either side, their leaves bursting with snippets of orange and yellow and crimson, shading the interior and casting it in shadow. Different from the other times I was here, when the pink and violet flowers of spring were in full bloom and the trees were richly verdant, but just as spectacular.

The cabin looks exactly as I remember it, as if time has stood still. I'm not sure that's a good thing. I suppose I'll find out soon enough. The style is Adirondack rustic, a sort of cross between a Swiss chalet and a log cabin on the prairie. The Great Camp dwellings are, by design, rustic and basic, but made of the finest natural materials, in a no-frills style that intentionally thumbs its nose at pretense. The opposite of the way the wealthy were living in the city back when they were built, which was the whole point.

The Parker camp is not overly large. Maybe two thousand square feet? A dark wood exterior with stone pillars frames a cozy front porch with rocking chairs and a swing. A railing made of bark and twigs blends with the surrounding bushes and trees. Dark red paint for the trim adds a touch of whimsy. A stone chimney born of the mountain rock funnels down to the massive fireplace inside, the only source of heat. Originally, it was an A-frame two-bedroom, one bath, but they've added on an additional master bedroom, giving it an eclectic feel that matches the interior, from what I remember. I'm surprised they didn't add a second bath. Perhaps that's a more complicated undertaking. I don't think they're on a public sewer line.

In keeping with the spirit of the retreat lifestyle, no

internet service and no TV. It does have electricity and running water. You don't come for the glam. It's all about nature, which I'm not too keen on—and I love my internet access.

My college friends and I haven't seen each other in ten years, and it has me feeling a little panicky, like we won't know what to say after so much time. And that we can't simply cue up a movie or glue ourselves to our computers and pretend we have work to do if we have nothing to say to one another. It's been a long time, and people change.

But then, we all needed to change.

For the first two years of college, the six of us were inseparable. Just six partier misfits who had, by some miracle, managed to gain admission to a good school and viewed it as an opportunity to test the limits of human endurance. If there had been an Olympics of partying back then, some kind of team sport obstacle course of beer bongs and shots and pot and pills, we'd have been some serious contenders for a gold medal. I'm surprised we all made it out alive.

Well, not Lanie.

Lanie didn't make it out alive.

But by senior year, we'd all mellowed. Gotten more serious about our studies. Except for Ted, who'd dropped out and started to work construction. But he stayed part of the group, because by that time, he was Ella's boyfriend. Now, they're married.

Lanie was the biggest waste case in those early days, aside from me, but also the one who turned herself around the most. She'd been raised by foster parents and Ella sort of took her in. Ella came from money. Not billionaire money, but compared to the rest of us, she was well off. Ella brought

Lanie home for Thanksgiving when she didn't have a place to go. Took her under her wing. That sort of thing.

But by senior year, Lanie had really cleaned up her act. After her internship, the summer between junior and senior year, Lanie was more focused on her career than any of us, aside from Brainy, the premed guy. That's why it's so hard for me to believe that she got wasted enough to walk off a cliff and tumble down a mountain to her death.

But what do I know?

If only I'd stayed coherent that night. That weekend was a setback for me, and I'm not proud of it. One last night of total abandon before I graduated and became a real adult. I'd already started dating Matt, who went to the same college but didn't hang out with us. Straightlaced, driven, focused Matt.

Everything I needed.

But what of my wants?

I stop to send a text to Matt that I've arrived.

There's a text message from him on my phone.

> Keep an eye on the weather. That hurricane has shifted.

I heard yesterday that there was a hurricane. Headed up the coast. Approaching Virginia, I think? Why would it affect us this deep into New York State? Matt can be like that. He worries too much. He's probably sandbagging the house right now.

Still, we're bound to get a lot of rain, which means we could get stuck in the cabin together, rather than being able to spread out on the grounds and go for a solitary hike or run. That might feel weird, after all these years.

When I text Matt back, the message doesn't go through. I knew they had no internet, but is it possible we'll have no cell service too? I'm starting to have some serious second thoughts about this weekend.

Gathering my overnight bag, I take a deep breath, square my shoulders, and head in.

"REAGAN!" Ella comes running up to me like I've just returned from the dead. "How are you?" Her head tilts to one side as she eyes me with a look on her face that says: *Come here, you poor thing.*

I'm a train wreck, I know. Meanwhile, she looks great, like someone who comes from money always does. Her signature long blonde hair is cut to shoulder length now but it's just as smooth and silky. A few crow's feet around her hazel eyes give her face character. Otherwise, she looks the same.

She has two kids under five, but you'd never know it. I suspect she had a mommy makeover or whatever it is women do to put themselves back together after birthing two kids. Or maybe she just hit the gym hard and started eating right, something I should do, but then that's never been high on my list of priorities. I could learn a few things from Ella.

"My little contribution to our weekend gathering," I say.

She takes the paper bag and looks inside. "Oh, did you bake these for us?"

"Yep. Chocolate chip scones. Your favorite."

"They smell delicious, and you are too bad! I'm trying to do low carb, no sugar," she says.

Of course she is.

"Oh, well, I—"

"I'm just teasing you, Reagan. We're not nineteen anymore, though. But this is a special occasion."

Then she eyes me with a sly look on her face. "Wait. They're not, you know? Your special scones?"

"What? No, Ella. I'm a responsible adult now. Don't worry."

"Oh, no judgement, Reagan. Everyone's doing the gummy thing now. I didn't mean anything by it."

Yeah, right.

There's always been a bit of underlying tension between Ella and me, and I need to check myself on my cattiness. Because of the unspoken competition between Lanie and me for her attention, and also because Ted and I made out once, well before he and Ella got together. It was no big deal, and it came out much later, after they'd been together for about a year.

But it may have been a big deal to Ella, because if I'm being honest, I kind of knew she liked him, even back in freshman year. I was immature. She had this way of giving me little digs now and then, and she seemed to be dumping me a little for Lanie. And although I wasn't conscious of it at the time, I may have kissed him simply to put her in her place.

It was Lanie who let it slip a few years later. Ella had been complaining about Ted letting his studies slide. "Aren't you glad you dodged that bullet?" Lanie said to me, in front of Ella, maybe because we both thought she could do better.

It was a stupid thing to say. Or maybe Lanie wasn't being stupid. Maybe she wanted to put a rift between Ella and me.

As I said, with a three-way friendship between young women, there's always some tension and competition, and both Lanie and I vied for Ella's attention.

None of us understood Ella's attraction to Ted, an Albany debutante and a soon-to-be college dropout. Ted's attractive, don't get me wrong. Tall, with a solid build. Dark wavy hair. A nice smile. A hunk, if you will. But we figured Ella would go for someone more like her, from an established family. The preppy country club type, which Ted wasn't, at least back then. Perhaps he's changed.

By that time, I was already dating Matt, a business major with an eye on an MBA program after college. With my track record, I knew I needed someone solid and reliable.

After Lanie's comment about Ted and me, Ella shot up from the sofa. "What the hell does that mean?"

I confessed that we'd had one stupid make-out session, back in the early part of sophomore year, before they had even gotten together, right before I started seeing Josh. She calmed down pretty quickly, but I swear she never looked at me the same way again. Ella is not the kind of person who likes to play second chair to anyone. From then on, I watched myself around Ted.

He seems to feel the same way, even ten years later. He doesn't hug me, but rather stands next to Ella and offers me a polite wave of his hand as he greets me.

"Hey, Reagan," he says.

"Great to see you, Ted."

They show me to my room, and I spend more time than is reasonable getting settled in. It's awkward with just the three of us here. It's Friday afternoon, and people have to work, I guess. After fifteen minutes or so, I hear a car drive up. When I exit my room, Brainy comes running up to me and hugs me. He's six-four—lean and lanky—and he bends down and envelopes me in his arms.

"Reagan! I've missed you so much."

His hug feels genuine and warm.

"I've missed you, too," I say.

I don't address him by name, because I'm not sure if he still likes to be called Brainy or if he ever liked it at all. But somehow Brady feels too formal and unfamiliar. I decide I'll wait and see how the others handle it and follow suit. He's a gentle soul with a brilliant mind, one of those people with a freakishly high IQ who's a little short on social skills. He's married to another doctor, a surgeon named Pete whom I've never met. This is a no-spouse weekend, Ella decided. Ted's an exception because he's part of our original group.

"Where's Josh?" I ask.

"Running late," Ted says, and he rolls his eyes. "As usual."

Ted gives us a rundown on Josh, and it's not very flattering. He's single, and has been bouncing from job to job. I sense he may be exaggerating, although I hope not. Josh had the hots for Ella before she and Ted got together, and there's always been a bit of tension between Ted and Josh, so I take it with a grain of salt.

Although we thought Ted was an odd choice for a woman like Ella ten years ago, it seems to have worked out. He wasn't much for academia, but he's apparently a savvy businessman. He's built a virtual construction empire, in no small part due to the patronage of Ella's father, a successful real estate developer. Ted may be a lumberjack on the inside, but on the outside, he seems to be playing his part. If I didn't know better, I'd take him for a silver spoon blue blood—but maybe one with a personal trainer.

Ted and Ella are living large in upstate New York—a Saratoga Springs power couple—and it seems to have worked out for them. The two of them have box seats at the Saratoga Race Course. She's posted photos of them seated in the prestigious Founders Room on her social media. I suspect her parents got them in there, but maybe not. The implication is clear, though. They've arrived.

Just then, Josh enters and my stomach lurches. He and I were an item for a short time sophomore year, and I'm sorry to admit that he still has an effect on me. It's not that I still like him, or that I wish we were together. It's that being around him makes me uncomfortable. He brings out my insecurities. Reminds me of a time when my self-esteem was at a low point—and he helped it hit rock bottom.

I fell hard for him. Then he dumped me for Lanie. And to add insult to injury, after he broke up with me, he treated me like dirt. He'd mock me and give me crap about my drinking. Point out my flaws. It was weird. You'd think I broke up with him, not the other way around. It was as if it embarrassed him, the fact that we'd once been together. I have to admit, I was a little out of control. But we were friends first, and I didn't understand why he treated me that way.

Then a short time later, Josh dumped Lanie, too. He's still like that, from what I've heard. Not marriage material, and I should be grateful that it didn't work out. And I am, I guess.

I wish I looked better, though, which is a shitty thought to have. I'm a married woman. Although it makes me feel a little guilty, I tell myself there's no harm in that. Nobody wants to run into an ex when they look like crap. There won't be a repeat of the last time I saw him ten years ago, that's for sure. When I planted a kiss on him and he pushed me away.

And I popped a molly in my mouth.

SEVEN
ELLA

Ella hasn't been back to her family's camp since that fateful night ten years ago, and it's even weirder than she'd imagined it would be, seeing these people again. Ted took everyone for a quick look around the grounds, leaving her to prepare dinner for them.

At the moment, Ella's questioning her bright idea to gather them for a little reunion. It's a risk getting everyone together like this. But it's a risk she's prepared to take. She'd secretly been hoping her parents would sell the place, but so far that hasn't happened. At least she's found a use for it.

Her brother and his family use the property a few times a year, and her mother and father live about an hour away, so they sometimes come up for the day. But mostly it sits empty, and as she runs a finger over the cracked brown leather sofa in desperate need of repair, her mind flashes back to better days. The days before she got the bright idea freshman year to host her college friends for a weekend of parting and debauchery.

When Ella was a child, she lived for their family trips to the camp. Not because she liked to hike or cross-country ski or hunt; she's not big on the outdoors. But because they were at their best up here. Her father is a workaholic, a serious man. But up here, he would lighten up. With no TV and no internet access, the four of them would play board games and cards and laugh and joke. Winter or summer, the evenings were what she enjoyed the most.

After an exhausting summer hike replete with bug bites and sweat and sore muscles, they'd get back to the cabin and chow on burgers washed down with iced tea. Her mother even let them eat with their hands up here, unlike at home where dinner was a formal affair and they had to put their napkins on their laps and use the proper fork for their salads.

Ella dreaded the bitter cold and the cross-country skiing excursions in the winter when the air was so frigid it hurt to breathe in. But she loved the feeling of returning to the warm cabin, making a blazing fire, and drinking hot chocolate with marshmallows. It was as if the moment they walked through the door, they could shed all the pretense and just be a regular family. And now those memories are forever tainted by Lanie's death and Ella's bad decisions.

The five of them come back in, and Ted sees them to their rooms. Josh and Brady will share the bunk bed room, Ella and Ted will take the master, and Reagan can have a room to herself. She needs a good night's sleep. Ella expected her to look worse, frankly, from what Matt said. She could use a haircut and she's still got some baby weight on her, but other than that, she looks okay. Ella noticed the way Reagan looked at Josh, and she hopes she's not still carrying a torch for him. Hopefully, she's not foolish enough to act on it. Not like she did ten years ago, almost blowing it with Matt.

"Dinner's almost ready," Ella calls out to Ted.

Ted helps her set the table, and Ella tends to the food. It's a simple meal. Baked salmon with roasted potatoes and a salad. Soon, the five of them are seated around the rustic farmhouse table. Ted and Ella at the head and foot, Reagan and Brady on one side, and Josh across from them. The meal is served family style, and everyone seems reluctant to be the first to dig in.

"Please," Ella says. "Help yourselves."

Josh shrugs and goes for the salmon. "Looks great, Ella. Thanks."

Soon the others follow suit.

It's painfully awkward, until everyone gets a little wine in them. Then things start to flow a little.

"Remember the first time we all came up here? Freshman year?" Ted says.

"Like it was yesterday," Josh says.

Ella remembers, too. The first time was the best time. A good memory. It had taken a while for her to find a group of friends she felt comfortable with. She was popular in high school. Not quite a mean girl, but close.

Lanie was her roommate freshman year, and they couldn't have been from more different backgrounds. Back then, people didn't say things like *check your privilege*. But that's exactly what rooming with Lanie made her do. Her college professors filled her mind and opened her eyes, and she saw herself in a different light. Spoiled and clueless, with no hardship stories to tell.

Reagan wasn't as wealthy as Ella, but she wasn't like

Lanie either. Sort of in the middle. But Reagan had a bohemian air about her that Ella found intriguing. Plus, Reagan and Lanie grew close, so she didn't have much choice but to embrace a friendship with Reagan, although there was always a little competition between Ella and Reagan for Lanie's attention. That changed after Josh dumped Reagan for Lanie, late in sophomore year.

But that was later. After the first gathering, which was the best one. The six of them were platonic at that point, but over the years, that changed, making everything more complicated. And eventually, both Reagan and Lanie betrayed her. Lanie's betrayal stung the most, after everything she'd done for her.

But at least Ella no longer feels guilty about her privilege.

Ella attempts to get the conversation going, trying to bring them back to happier times when they were young and innocent. "The first year was the best one," she says.

"Didn't you smoke pot and get all panicky, Brainy?" Josh asks.

Typical Josh, picking on Brady. But she needs him here this weekend, just like she needs Reagan. Poor Brady's sort of along for the ride.

Brady glares at Josh. "Nobody calls me that anymore."

Josh dismisses his comment. "Awe, lighten up, dude."

Ella sees Brady's nostrils flare, which makes her smile a little. Josh was kind of an asshole to Brady back in college, and he took it. It's nice to see him starting to stick up for himself, and she's eager for Josh to get what's coming to him.

Ted turns to Josh. "I seem to remember you hurling in the yard."

Ella's pleased with her husband for coming to Brady's rescue.

"Guilty," Josh says. "I own my screw-ups."

Reagan chimes in, trying to put Josh in his place. "Are you implying that the rest of us don't?" Reagan quips.

"I'm not the one who fell in a fire," Josh shoots back at her.

"That wasn't the first year," Brady points out. "Ella asked about the first year, Josh."

They're silent for a bit, the thickening tension in the air starting to make Ella nervous. It's very early in the weekend, and she doesn't need everyone ganging up on Josh. That's not part of the plan, but he's sort of asking for it.

Wisely, Ted changes the subject. "So, enough about the past. What've you all been up to the last ten years?"

They fill each other in on the highlights. Ted and Ella have their construction business and two kids. Brady's a doctor, married to another one. Reagan and Matt have a baby, and she's taking time off from her marketing job. And then there's Josh. Still single, bouncing from job to job, the latest being a sales position for a solar company.

As the guests finish dinner and head over to the living area with their wine, Ella and Ted clear the table.

Ted's phone buzzes.

He glances down at it.

"Oh damn," he says.

"What?" Ella asks.

"That hurricane. It's gotten stronger and wider. They think we might get some heavy rain and even some wind, starting tomorrow night. But they're not sure. It says to take precautions."

"Maybe we should do the service in the morning and cut the weekend short," Reagan calls out from the sofa.

"It'll probably be fine," Josh says. "We're pretty far inland."

But Ella knows better. If the storm shifts, the roads could become unpassable. It happened before, with Irene, over a decade ago, and with Beryl, more recently.

"We'll keep an eye on it," Ted says.

And as they wind up their evening, a sinking feeling settles in the pit of Ella's stomach with the oily salmon. A strange mixture of anger, remorse—and dread.

EIGHT
REAGAN

The evening was weird and uncomfortable, and I'm happy that I'm finally in my own room, away from all of them. There are only three bedrooms at the cabin, and I'm lucky to have the smallest one to myself. Ted and Ella have the master, and Brainy and Josh were supposed to share the bunk beds in the bigger guest room, but that's not how it worked out.

Poor Brainy.

At least one good thing has already come from this gathering.

I no longer give a crap what Josh Tanner thinks of me.

It's amazing what ten years of maturity can do to a person. Sure, he still has that boyish charm with his windswept hair and those disarmingly darling dimples, and if he was an actor in a movie, I'd put him on my list of hot celebrities I'm allowed to sleep with. But he's a major asshole. Why didn't I see that ten years ago?

First, the minute he entered the cabin, he went straight

to Brainy and patted him on the back, using his nickname, of course, insensitive clod that he is. When Brady protested, Josh laughed it off. Come to think of it, Josh is the one who gave him the nickname to begin with. Then Josh made a weird comment about the sleeping arrangements, which was offensive and downright homophobic, although I think he was trying to make a joke.

Brainy and Josh were roommates freshman year, so maybe Josh thought they were close enough for him to get away with it, but it didn't land well. I offered to stay in the bunk bed room with Brainy—*Brady,* I remind myself—but he said he'd sleep in the living room.

"I was only joking, Brainy," Josh said. "I'm cool with sharing."

Brady narrowed his eyes at Josh. "It's Brady," he said.

Then he stared Josh down until Josh looked away.

I guess I'm not the only one who's changed. Brady would never have stood up to Josh like that back in college, and if I were Josh, I'd watch it. He might be cute, but he's a smaller guy. If Brady wanted to, he could pulverize Josh Tanner. Still, Josh didn't get the message, and I have to wonder if that slipup at dinner was intentional or if he's simply that clueless.

I'm starting to think this gathering was a very bad idea. Our friendships years ago were based on nothing more than teen rebellion and a lust for adventure, and most of our time together was spent in a haze of alcohol and drug-induced, *Fear and Loathing in Las Vegas*-inspired abandon. I realize that I don't know these people very well. I don't know their values or their vices, or who they are at their cores.

Could one of them have pushed Lanie down into that ravine?

Sure. I didn't think so before, but I realize now that anything is possible.

Another thing I sense is that Ella has an agenda. She didn't bring us here to memorialize Lanie Martin. She's barely come up in conversation. Maybe Ella knows I saw something that night. Or maybe she thinks one of the others saw something.

It was Ella who was eager to put a lid on the investigation. Perhaps there's something she wants to keep hidden. It would come back to Ella and her parents if that biker guy had harmed Lanie. They're lucky that Lanie had no family to speak of, because even if it wasn't murder, they could still have been sued for allowing the raging party to happen on their property.

A raging party that led to a death.

And I already told Ella that I saw the biker guy try to chat up Lanie, the one who kissed me, but she forbade me from telling her parents or the police. I'm sure I could get in trouble for withholding that, so even if I wanted to come clean about that now, it's probably not the best idea. One thing's for sure, though. I need to watch my back.

I'm thirsty, so I sneak out into the living room and see that Brady's sleeping on the sofa. I tiptoe over to the kitchen area, trying to be quiet. It seems like they haven't upgraded the furniture or done any work to it in the last ten years. The same brown leather sofa, worn tan recliner, and light brown armchairs surround the wood slab coffee table. It's a big, open concept A-frame wooden structure with light wood paneling, exposed beams and older flooring. The floorboards creak under my feet, despite my efforts to tread lightly. With all the money they seem to have, I'm surprised they haven't fixed the place up over the years. Perhaps they don't use it much anymore, tainted as it is by the accident.

The interior is eclectic, as I recalled. Rich person eclectic. Trying to make it look as if the bearskin rug, the Hudson River School oil painting above the stone fireplace, and the artifacts from every continent save Antarctica weren't signifiers of excess, simply because they're strewn about a log cabin in a devil-may-care fashion. I'm surprised they haven't been burglarized. Maybe they're all knockoffs. What do I know?

"I'm up," Brady says.

"Sorry," I whisper. "I need a glass of water."

"I'm not tired," he says.

"Me either. You want some water?" I ask.

He motions to a black canister on the coffee table. "I'm good."

Then he sits up, as if he's inviting me to join him.

I walk over toward him with my ice water. "So," I say.

He sighs. "It's a little weird, being back here," Brady says.

"It's *a lot* weird." I smile.

We both chuckle, and I take a seat on the worn beige recliner across from the brown leather sofa.

"So, how've you been, Doctor?" I ask. Truthfully, he's my favorite of the group, but that's not saying much. "You did it."

He smiles. "I did. Got a pile of debt to show for it, too."

"Well, that sucks."

"It's part of the deal. Unless you have rich parents or

you're dirt poor. The middle class gets the squeeze these days."

"One of us is doing well. I noticed a Tesla truck parked outside when I went to get my glasses out of the car before I went to bed. Is it yours?" I ask Brady.

"No, are you kidding? With my mountain of student loan debt? I drive the aging Honda Pilot. Josh drives the Tesla," Brady says. "Claims he needs it for work."

"Josh can afford a Tesla?" I say. "I thought Ted said Josh was floundering."

Brady shrugs. "He said he had some kind of side gig, on top of his solar sales job. But I bet it's leased. And you? You're a mom now. How's that going? How's Matt?"

I sigh, and for some reason, I have a need to let my guard down. To unload all my baggage on Brady, who's always been a good listener.

"It's been a struggle, to tell you the truth. I've been having some issues. Postpartum depression, they tell me. I thought getting away would do me some good."

"Oh, I'm so sorry about that, Reagan. Don't blame yourself. It's your hormones. I'm an endocrinologist, so I'm not just saying it. It's true."

"I've always struggled with anxiety, which I think you know. And I'm sure that was part of why I was such a waste case back then. But depression? That's a new one for me."

Brady hung with us back then, but he was more of an observer than a participant. He drank a little but never did drugs, and I'm sure he's armed with a repository of embarrassing stories about all of us that he could unleash at any time. The rest of us were probably too plastered to remember much of anything, unflattering or otherwise.

"Don't blame yourself. Mental illness is tough to treat, and there's still a lot of stigma around it. It's getting better, but society is not there yet. You self-medicated, which happens a lot when people have a mental illness."

Mental illness?

Do they all think of me as the mentally ill one?

My eyes narrow on him. "I'm not mentally ill, Brady. I just have anxiety. It's pretty common."

"Oh, I didn't mean it like that, Reagan." His eyes look as if they're about to water, and suddenly I see the Brainy from ten years ago. "Please don't be mad at me."

I shake my head. "I'm not mad at you, Brady. It's fine. I know you're trying to make me feel better."

"I didn't mean anything by it." He shrugs.

"It's fine. Don't worry."

"How's married life?" I ask.

Brady shrugs. "It's good, but busy. With both of us starting out in our careers, it's hard to get a lot of quality time together. But that's the deal. We knew that going in. And it's not going to change, so we need to make it work."

I nod along. "Yeah, quality time is hard to come by for us, too. A baby changes everything. Mostly in a good way, but I know what you mean."

Brady purses his lips. "So why are we both here, instead of on some romantic getaway with our spouses?"

"I felt like I needed to come. Like I owed it to Lanie," I say. I'm not about to tell him the real reason. That I'm here trying to remember something that might be better left forgotten.

"Yeah, me too," he says.

I wonder if Brady feels guilty, too. Probably, he does. An

awkward silence follows, and I want to get us back on track. I need an ally this weekend, and Brady's my best bet.

"Want to know a secret?" I ask.

Brady's brows rise. "Sure."

"I think Josh Tanner is a jackass."

He nods. "A total jackass. Always was. But I worshipped him back in college. Don't get the wrong idea. He's not my type, as far as romance. I wasn't attracted to him or anything. But I had a hard time making friends, and he helped me meet people. He's so charismatic. It's effortless for him. I thought it would rub off on me. I knew he was getting laughs at my expense back then, but I let it happen."

I shrug. "Well, you stood up for yourself tonight, and I doubt he'll be making those kinds of cracks anymore. I was taken by him too, back then. I had a hard time getting over our little fling, which is embarrassing for me to admit now. What did I see in him? I guess you and I have matured. Not sure about the others."

"Yeah, I know you had a hard time, Reagan. You tried to kiss him that last night at the camp, but he pushed you away. And then later that night, he started chatting up Lanie, and you were really pissed off."

My heart is immediately in my throat.

I was mad at Lanie that night?

I remember trying to kiss Josh, but that was only to stave off the biker guy, and I tell Brady that. I have no memory of being upset with Lanie, so I protest. Maybe Brady has it wrong. "I wasn't mad at Lanie, Brady. Not at all. I was worried about her. Because some biker guy was hitting on her. The same one who hit on me."

"Well, that might be true. There were a bunch of bikers

there. But I wasn't drinking much, and you were out of your mind that night. And I'm telling you, you were hopping mad when you saw Josh talking to Lanie. I was standing next to you. They walked off toward the woods. You grabbed my arm and called Lanie a bitch. Then you stormed off. I remember being surprised because you were dating Matt already, and I thought you two were going strong."

I take a deep breath as my mind swirls and my world shifts on its axis.

Why don't I remember this?

Struggling for a way out, because I know how it looks, I try to frame it in a way that seems the least damaging. "Maybe I was confused," I say. "I was wasted. Maybe I didn't remember I was with Matt, and I thought Josh and I were still together."

It's possible. We were together once, the second time we camped out on the mountain, sophomore year, when he broke it off with me and hooked up with Lanie.

Brady gives me an out. "Sure, Reagan. That could be. The ecstasy messes with your memory and your mind. That's certainly possible. I'm glad you're over Josh now, and that you ended up with Matt. He's a great guy."

"Yeah, me too, Brady. Matt's great."

We continue to make small talk and I feign normalcy, but a sinking feeling settles in the pit of my stomach.

I was mad at Lanie the night she died?

Suddenly, I'm not so eager to unearth those buried memories.

NINE
ELLA

Ella slips out of bed while Ted snores away next to her. He's not particularly loud; his repertoire is more like heavy breathing with an occasional snort or gasp, but it was enough to wake her up. She's never been a very sound sleeper.

At first, Ted didn't love this idea. But when he realized it presented an opportunity to take care of another pressing problem, he grew to like it, even though she started to have second thoughts. And now, she senses that Ted's holding back something, and she doesn't like it. Ella's the kind of woman who likes to be in control. So far, Ted has been the perfect match for her, content to live under the shadow of her well-connected family and her father's patronage.

Ella manages the money and the business part of their construction company; Ted does all the hard work. Vice President, she calls herself. This gives her some status in the community, but also leaves her unencumbered by a full-time job or other weighty responsibilities that would be an unnecessary distraction, allowing her to steer their ship in the direction she needs it to go.

Brady's sleeping on the sofa, she sees.

Damn that Josh Tanner.

He's such a blowhard.

Back in college, all of them treated Josh like he was some kind of rock star. Lanie and Ella both vying for his affection. Poor Brady, scarfing up the scraps Josh fed him while he got laughs at Brady's expense. Josh made a play for her once, but she shot him down. He's not Ella's type at all. She likes to be the center of attention. It never would have worked with Josh.

But Ted has always been a little jealous of Josh, and there's some tension between the two of them, even to this day. She's sure Ted knew that Josh hit on her. Why wouldn't he? He hit on everyone.

It's easy for Ella to see why Ted thought this was a bad idea—because it is. None of these people are her friends. Not anymore. Maybe they never were. But it's not like she has much choice. Loose ends are dangerous for her.

And there are a lot of loose ends from the night Lanie Martin died.

Ella puts on a pot of coffee as quietly as possible, so as not to wake Brady. Not only for his sake but for hers. It's just before dawn, and she needs some time alone, to process what happened last night and assess the situation.

Reagan is a problem. She's clearly unstable. In addition to the memories resurfacing, Matt revealed that Reagan tried to kill herself in her postpartum state, but he asked her not to say anything to Reagan about it. Ella promised to keep a close watch on her.

"Hey, Ella," Brady says, stretched out on the sofa, peeking out from under a pile of colorful, patterned woolen blankets.

"Oh, sorry I woke you," Ella replies.

So much for quiet reflection.

"It's fine. I got six hours, which is a lot for me. In my profession, I've learned to function on very little sleep."

"I'm sure," Ella says. "Coffee?" she asks.

"Yes, please. Black," Brady says.

"It'll just be a few minutes," Ella says.

Brady turns away from her and faces the back of the sofa.

After a few minutes, the smell of freshly brewed coffee starts to fill the space around her, and a hint of light peaks through the darkness. Ella can see the faint outline of trees outside the window. It's a densely wooded area, and she's often wondered whether they shouldn't cut back the foliage a bit, given the more recent dangers of forest fires that seem to come out of nowhere and strike in the most unlikely of places. And if that hurricane hits, the trees might be a problem. A few years ago, one crashed down onto the cabin, caving in part of the roof. And it wasn't even a bad storm.

Ella doctors up her coffee and delivers a mug of steaming hot black coffee to Brady, who by this time is sitting up. He looks good, and she's pleased that he's learned to assert himself. It always bothered her that Brady took so much crap from Josh when they were younger, and she's a little disappointed in herself that she didn't stick up for him back then. She'd felt mature as a college student, but looking back, Ella can see that she still had one foot in middle school; she wasn't confident enough back then to challenge a guy like Josh.

"So, how did you sleep? Sorry about Josh. He's the one who should be sleeping on the couch."

"It's fine," Brady says. "Those bunk beds are a little short for me, anyway."

"So, how's married life?" she asks.

"Good, but we're both so busy."

"I can imagine."

"I'm not sure you can," Brady says. "You're not a doctor."

Ella presses her lips. "*Hmm.* I suppose that's true. And you used the little time you have to come here and get slapped in the face by Josh."

Brady shrugs. "I liked Lanie a lot. I wanted to come."

"I'm sure that wherever she is, she knows that."

"I don't believe in that, Ella. But it's fine if you do."

Ella knows that Reagan and Brady were out here talking last night. She woke up for a short time and heard some murmuring, enough to know whose voices she was hearing, but she couldn't make out what they were saying. She wonders if Brady knows about Ella's incident, or if she's the only one privy to this information.

"Well, just the same, I want to do something for her this weekend. I'm having flowers delivered, and I thought we'd all go to the ravine and place them there. And maybe I'd say a little prayer, if that doesn't bother you."

Brady's brow furrows. "Why would it bother me? I just told you, whatever you believe is fine with me."

Ella decides to give Brady an opening to disclose what he knows, in case Reagan confided in him. "I hope it doesn't trigger anything for Reagan. She's kind of fragile, and I wasn't even sure she'd come."

"She was close to Lanie. Why wouldn't she come?" Brady says.

"She just had a baby. And between you and me, she's been having some issues."

"I know, Ella. Reagan told me. Postpartum depression. It's common, and it'll pass."

"It's not common to try and kill yourself," Ella quips.

Brady's eyes widen. "Reagan tried to kill herself? How do you know this?"

"Matt called and told me. He asked me to reach out to her. And when I did, Reagan told me she'd been thinking a lot about Lanie over the summer, ever since the baby was born. So, I got the idea to host this gathering, hoping that it might help her process what happened. Help all of us, really. We were all traumatized. I feel guilty. Reagan feels guilty. We all do. It's only natural. But we were young and stupid, and I thought if we got together now that we've matured, maybe we could help each other heal."

"Well, most of us have matured." Brady smiles.

"Right," Ella says. "I should have left Josh off the invite list."

"Nah." Brady waves off her comment. "It's fine. It wouldn't be the same without him."

Ella's comment was just for show.

She needs Josh to be here this weekend.

As if on cue, Josh bursts out the door of the bunk bed room.

"Morning, glories," Josh says, eyeing them with a sly grin on his face. "Rise and shine." He stretches and forces a yawn. "Coffee?" Josh asks.

"In the kitchen," Ella says.

Josh heads over to the cabinet, grabs a mug, and pours himself a cup. "You got any sugar?" he asks.

Ella shakes her head. "No, sorry. I don't think we do. But there's some creamer in the fridge that might sweeten it a bit."

"Good enough." He reaches into the fridge for the creamer.

Then Josh saunters over to the sofa with his coffee and plops down next to Brady. "I'll take the sofa tonight, Brady. I'm sorry I acted like such a tool. I guess I just slipped back into my old habits."

Brady shrugs. "Sure, Josh."

"*Bad* habits, I mean." Josh looks earnest now. "I'm really sorry, dude. It won't happen again."

"It's fine," Brady says. "I don't want to talk about it anymore."

It's not lost on Ella that Josh finally dropped the nickname.

"So, what's on the agenda for the day?" Josh asks.

Ella lets out a huff and her hands fly up into the air. "The memorial service? For Lanie? It's why we're here, Josh." She shakes her head.

"I know that, Ella. But we're not doing that all day long. Let's organize a hike or something. We can't sit around all day and mope. Lanie was fun. She wouldn't want that, and you know it."

"I guess you have a point," Ella says. "I'll go check on Ted. We can let Reagan sleep. She probably needs it."

Lanie *was* fun, Ella thinks. That was part of her problem. Too much fun. Shy at first glance, but she had a way of endearing herself to people, and she wasn't as innocent as she seemed. Her dark, soulful eyes turned heads away from Ella and toward her. Combined with her "tragic" past, Lanie got a lot of attention from everyone in Ella's life.

Too much attention.

Ella leaves the former roommates to find their groove, pleased that Josh's tune has changed. It's an act, she figures. But Josh and Brady's relationship is not her biggest concern right now. She's concerned about Reagan, and why Lanie's on her mind now, after all these years. Maybe it's the anniversary, or maybe it's something else.

But whatever it is, it can't be good.

As Ella walks to her bedroom, she hears Josh excuse himself to use the shower.

So much for finding their groove.

If she can get through the ceremony without any further drama, they can wrap up the weekend and put this entire sordid mess to rest, once and for all.

At least, that's the plan.

TEN
REAGAN

Brady is sitting up on the sofa when I come out of my bedroom. Sleep finally came, and I actually got more of it than I normally do at home these days. Danny stays down for longer stretches now, but he vocalizes a lot more, and although he's in the next room, the baby monitor sits on my nightstand, so I still wake up a lot, even if he doesn't. I called Matt last night and he assured me that all is well. He seems to be doing fine without me, and I wonder if I should be concerned about that.

"Hey, are we the first ones up?" I ask.

"No," Brady says. "Ella woke me up. She made coffee, if you want it." He motions to the kitchen. "Josh went to take a shower."

"How are things with him this morning?" I ask.

He shrugs. "Fine. He apologized again. And he seemed to mean it this time."

"Good."

The smell of coffee hits me, and I crave it in my bones.

One positive consequence of moving to formula. I can drink it guilt free now, as much as I want. Plus, it made this trip a lot easier, not having to pump and store breast milk. And I feel like now that I've totally weaned Danny, my hormones are more stable. I'm getting there.

Finally.

I hope this weekend isn't going to cause a setback.

"How did you sleep?" Brady asks, as I sit across from him with my coffee mug.

"Great," I tell him. "Better than I have in ages. I feel like a new person. Thanks for the talk."

"Yeah, sleep deprivation can really exacerbate the hormone stuff," he says. "Don't push yourself this weekend, Reagan. Take it easy."

My eyes widen. "What's that supposed to mean?"

Brady's looking at me differently than he did last night. I wonder what's changed.

He bristles. "Um, I mean, be careful, that's all."

"Be careful about what?" I ask.

Brady is fidgeting now, rubbing his thighs with his hands. He stalls before he answers me. "It's a difficult weekend, that's all I'm saying. For all of us. So watch yourself. Especially after what you've been through."

Does he think I'll get drunk again or something?

My eyes narrow on him. "Brady, I'm not going to do anything crazy. I hardly drink anymore."

He shakes his head. "That's not what I meant. I was talking about..."

"About?" I ask.

What is he getting at?

After taking a deep breath, he continues. "The postpartum stuff. The depression." His expression borders on pity.

"I told you. It's getting better," I say.

This is strange. He didn't look at me like that last night when I told him about the postpartum depression. What's changed? Did Ella put ideas in his head? That would be like her. I think Matt may have told her about the incident.

"Brady. Did Ella say something to you?" I ask.

He sighs. "Yeah, but don't tell her I told you. Please?"

I roll my eyes. "What exactly did she tell you, Brady?"

Brady looks away and then back to me. He blows out a breath. "She said you tried to kill yourself."

My eyes pop open. "What? That's not what happened at all! I didn't try to kill myself."

"You didn't?" he asks.

"No. I just got confused. I took a gummy that was too strong, to try and sleep. It interacted with my SSRI and another sedative I was on. I mean, yeah, I should have probably known better and it wasn't a great idea. But I didn't want to *kill* myself. Why would she say that?"

Brady looks genuinely puzzled, and I feel like he believes me. "I don't know, Reagan. You'd have to ask her," he says.

"Does everyone know about this?" I ask.

He shrugs. "No idea. I'm guessing Ted does. I don't know about Josh."

Suddenly, I want to leave this place. Get away from these people and their patronizing looks. Between the revelation that I was mad at Lanie ten years ago and the idea that everyone thinks I tried to kill myself, I'm starting to worry that this whole weekend is some kind of pity party for me.

But then, who gave Ella the idea that I purposely took a

dangerous drug combination? Did she come up with that on her own, or did Matt put the idea in her head?

And what about Matt?

My mother?

Does this mean they all doubt my claim that I didn't mean for it to happen?

Because I didn't mean for it to happen.

Did I?

I NEED A SHOWER, and I plan to get one before everyone uses up the hot water. I remember that being a bit of a problem. Gathering my things in my room, I head out and open the bathroom door.

"Hey," someone yells.

Oh my God.

It's Josh.

I slam the door shut—but not before seeing Josh in the full monty.

Leaning against the door, I struggle for a way to spin this that won't make me look like an idiot. Because this is a disaster. With his ego, he'll probably think I did it on purpose, just like that kiss ten years ago.

Sure enough, Josh comes out of the bathroom with a shit-eating grin on his face. "Well hello there, Reagan Carlson." He winks. "Don't worry, our secret's safe with me."

Speaking through gritted teeth, I correct him. "It's Reagan Hansen now."

He knows this.

And then I offer an apology, of sorts. "And I'm sorry I walked in on you. But why didn't you lock the door?"

Josh stands tall with a towel wrapped around his waist, sticking out his ripped pecs like a proud peacock. He's loving this. "The lock doesn't work," he says. "You're supposed to knock. That's the system. You know that, Reagan. What? Did you forget?"

I let out a sigh.

He's right.

"I forgot," I admit.

"Yeah, right." Josh scoffs. "You needed one last peek, admit it. No harm, no foul. It's not like we haven't seen each other's—"

Fury explodes in me like a match to a powder keg. For the way he treated me when we were together—and for the way I let myself be treated, during and after our brief romance. For the way he dumped me. For the way he failed to believe that I only kissed him ten years ago to get that guy to leave me alone. For the way he failed to protect me against the biker guy in the first place.

"Stop it, Josh! Just stop. You are a self-centered *jackass*! I can't believe I ever let you get your hooks in me. I didn't open the door on purpose. Just like I didn't kiss you ten years ago because I secretly wanted to get back with you. There's no excuse for the way you treated me when we went out, and the way you continually poured salt in the wound after we broke up. You owe me an apology. I was your friend first. What exactly did I ever do to you to make you treat me like that?"

Josh takes a step back, like he's afraid of me.

Good!

He should be.

"Look, Reagan," he says. "I've got a weird sense of humor. I joke around a lot, but I never meant to hurt your feelings. And if I did, I'm truly sorry."

"There's a fine line between joking and mocking someone," I point out. "If you're only getting laughs at someone else's expense, maybe you need to work on some new material. Look at the way you treated Brady all those years. And how you tried to treat him this weekend."

"Brady and I are fine," he says.

"I wouldn't be so sure about that," I shoot back.

His brows rise and his mouth opens, and he's about to speak, but I cut him off. "And what about the way you treated Lanie?"

"What about it?" he says.

"You dumped her, just like you dumped me."

"What are you talking about? Lanie dumped me. I would say she broke my heart, but according to you, I don't have one." He looks away, a hint of sadness in his eyes.

This is news to me, that Lanie dumped him, and it stops my anger in its tracks.

"Huh?" I say. "That's not what she told me. She said you dumped her, too."

His eyes narrow on me. "Lanie was a good person, Reagan. She probably said that so she wouldn't hurt your feelings. Unlike me, I guess. Cause I'm a...let's see if I've got this right. A callous jackass, incapable of caring about anyone but myself. Is that about it?"

Josh glares at me and it's clear I've gotten to him, but at least I'm no longer the butt of his jokes. But he is annoyed rather than infuriated, and there's a sadness sitting behind the anger.

Did Josh love Lanie?

I let out a long sigh. "You're right, Josh. Lanie was a good person. This weekend is about her. So, let's let bygones be bygones. I accept your apology."

Josh smirks. "Great. Now go take your meds, Reagan."

If I were a cartoon character, this would be the point where steam would billow out of my ears and nose. Same old Josh. He'll never change.

I would shoot back at him, but I don't want to give him the satisfaction of letting him know he got to me again. Instead, I push past him, enter the bathroom, and close the door behind me. I hope he's the one who falls off a cliff and breaks his neck this time.

And I have to stop myself from saying that out loud.

ELEVEN
REAGAN

It's been decided that we'll all go for a hike and then have our memorial service for Lanie. I'm showered and dressed, ready to start the day—and then get it over with.

We got through one night. Only one more to go, and then I can leave this place and its spotty, drug-induced memories behind. I've done a one-eighty in my thinking, and now I don't care to remember anything more about that night. I want to leave this place and forget all about these people and my past. Dedicate myself to Matt and Danny and my future. Pull myself together. Not go looking for problems.

But as much as I don't want to remember, little flashes of that weekend keep rising up and slapping me in the face. The time of year was late spring and the days were warm, about like it is this weekend, on the cusp of a new season. Evenings still got chilly, though, and I recall feeling too cold and going back into the cabin to get my jacket, when the evening revelry was just beginning. I think that's when they started the fire.

And when I entered the house, Ella was on a call. On their landline, which they still had back then. When I walked in, her head whipped around toward me and she stopped talking. Something had upset her, but it wasn't my coming into the house. Because I heard her as I walked in, talking to someone in a hushed but harried tone, like she would have been yelling if she didn't have to be worried about people overhearing her.

"Sorry," I mouthed. "Just getting my jacket."

She forced a smile and placed her hand over the phone's speaker. "No problem, Reagan." Then she told whoever she was talking to that she had to go and hung up. When I came out of my room with my jacket, she was gone.

Another memory flashes, from when I was relatively sober, if a bit hungover, the next day. Josh and Ella huddled together early the next morning as I glanced out the window.

I'm not sure why it's crossing my mind now, other than the fact that Brady brought up the issue of my getting upset at seeing Josh and Lanie.

Josh and Ella were outside the cabin on the front porch. I could see them through the window, in the midst of some kind of intense discussion. It seemed pretty intimate to me, like they were sharing a secret. I wondered if something was going on between the two of them. It was right before we started looking for Lanie; when we realized she was missing. When we began to realize that she wasn't in the cabin or with Josh.

One thing I know for certain is I wasn't feeling jealous or anything. Poor Ted, I remember thinking, if Ella was cheating. Which is weird, because Brady claims that I was upset about Josh hitting on Lanie the night before. I don't remember that at all. Maybe Brady misinterpreted what he saw? But then Brady said I called Lanie a bitch, and it's pretty hard to misinterpret that.

Perhaps that was at a different point in the evening, and the drugs were at full strength, messing with my mind and my memory. And at that point, I could have been confused and thought it was two years prior, the year when Josh dumped me for Lanie. I honestly don't remember being mad at Lanie, or what I could have been upset about. But I don't think it had anything to do with Josh.

Because when I saw Josh and Ella talking that morning, I distinctly remember missing Matt. By that point, the drugs had worn off. And one thing I know for sure is I wasn't upset or jealous at the thought of Josh and Ella at all. I wanted to leave and get back to Matt. I felt terribly guilty for trying to kiss Josh, and I was worried someone would tell Matt. Why would I be jealous of Lanie and Josh, but not Ella and Josh? None of this makes sense.

So, when I come out of my room now and see Josh and Ella huddled together again, ten years later, I do a double take. This time, though, it doesn't look amiable. More like they're upset with each other. Ella said something, but only part of it was audible to me.

Something about stopping?

When they realize I've entered the room, they spring back from each other once again. Just like ten years ago. What were they talking about? Were they rehashing an unfortunate indiscretion from a decade earlier? Could it still be going on?

"Reagan," Ella says. "We were just talking about the hike. Looks like we're going to get some residual rain from that hurricane that's coming up the coast. I think we need to cancel it, but Josh doesn't agree."

Ella shoots Josh a sideways glance.

Josh rolls his eyes.

"It's not due for a few hours," Josh says. "You worry too much. It'll be fine. It's not the storm. You just don't like hiking."

Ella shrugs.

It's true, ironically. Ella's not very outdoorsy, even though this is her family's cabin in the woods. We used to tease her about it. And I suppose this could be the reason I got that weird vibe from them. A disagreement about the day's agenda. But somehow, it seems like more than that.

"We decided we'll do the memorial service first. Then do the hike, if the weather holds out. That's why we're here, after all," Ella says.

Then she glares at Josh again.

"Yeah, I know, Ella. I'm fully aware of the reason we're all here," Josh shoots back.

The trouble is, they're not acting like two people who haven't seen each other for ten years. And if I didn't know better, I'd think I'd walked in on a married couple having a spat. Or at the very least, two extremely close friends. It seems almost impossible to me that they haven't been in touch for the last decade.

"Where's Ted?" I ask. "And Brady?"

"Ted ran to the store to get more supplies, in case that hurricane hits us. And Brady went for a run," Ella says.

Well, that's convenient.

Ella says to me, "And maybe you should touch base with Matt. It's veering toward Albany now."

Then Josh says he's going for a quick run, too, in case we can't go hiking later, leaving Ella and me in an uncomfortable silence. This is my chance to set her straight about my incident and the fact that I did not try to kill myself. Something holds me back, though. Perhaps it's better to just get through the weekend and move on, I decide.

I excuse myself to get ready for the hike to the ceremony site.

ABOUT FORTY MINUTES LATER, I hear a car drive up and feel like I can come out of my room. Ted's back, I assume, so it won't be just me and Ella. I couldn't reach Matt to ask him how they're doing. The service goes in and out, and I'm trying not to get concerned about that. There's a spot near the kitchen window that works pretty well, but I want to talk to my husband in private.

That hurricane wasn't a threat to us when I left, or I wouldn't have come here this weekend. I heard something about it the day before I left, but we're so far inland, I thought nothing of it. Funny he didn't mention it to me when we spoke. On the way up, the news reports said it was shifting in our general direction, but still, I didn't think much of it. We shouldn't get too much wind, but if we get a lot of rain, it could affect the roads here.

And with no internet service, I have no way of tracking it now. That makes me very nervous. Do we have enough provisions if we get stuck here a few days longer than we planned? I brought nothing with me, aside from the scones we've almost polished off already. Not even a granola bar or a bottle of water.

"Hi, honey," I hear a male voice say to Ella as I exit the bedroom.

But it's not Ted's voice.

It's an older man's voice.

It's vaguely familiar.

I come around the corner and see two people in the doorway. An older couple. It takes a few seconds for it to click it's been so long.

Ella's parents?

What in the hell are they doing here?

TWELVE
REAGAN

I expect her parents to walk over and embrace Ella, but instead, her mother comes rushing over to me like I'm Ella's long-lost twin who got separated at birth. She wraps her arms around me and pulls me in, holding me against her chest. I imagine her mouthing something to Ella, who's standing behind me, as she pats my back.

Good grief, Ella. She's such a mess.

Something like that.

She releases me, leans back, and looks me in the eye, keeping her hands planted on my shoulders. "Reagan! It's so lovely to see you after all these years. It's so nice that you two have kept in touch."

But we haven't really kept in touch. We were never that close to begin with.

What did Ella tell her?

And why is she making a fuss over me?

Then it hits me.

The pity party.

She must know about the incident.

I haven't asked Matt about it yet, about what he told Ella or why he gave her the impression that I tried to kill myself. I want to do it in private, and preferably not over the phone, so he can't weasel out of it. He's getting an earful when I get home, that's for sure. And so are my parents. I did not try to kill myself, I'm sure of it. And if that's the impression they got, I need to set everyone straight.

"Yes, it is, Mrs. Parker," I reply.

"Please, call me Helen," she insists. "And you remember Rob? My husband?"

"Sure," I say, fully incapable of addressing him by his first name. Ella's father is formal and distant, and I think I must have said a total of two words to the man my entire life. Why start now?

I'm saved by Ted coming in the front door. "I got a lot more food than we'll need for the weekend, just in case. And two more flashlights."

That makes me feel a little better.

Ella's father turns around to greet Ted and mentions something about having business to discuss. The two of them head into the kitchen with the shopping bags, leaving the three of us to make small talk. Then Ella's father comes back and mumbles something to his wife about Ted not having enough batteries for the flashlights. He says he's going back to the store to get some more, along with some supplies to replenish the first aid kit and a few fireplace logs that could offer more illumination.

It's painfully awkward for the first few minutes, and I think about faking stomach flu and heading out early. I'll see how I feel after the memorial service. I can't leave before then.

"We're only here for the service," Ella's mother says. "To pay our respects. Then we'll be out of your hair. I'm sure you kids have a lot of catching up to do."

That makes me feel a little better.

I think?

"Do you want some coffee, Mom?" Ella asks. "And one of Reagan's legendary chocolate chip scones?"

"Oh, that would be lovely," Helen replies.

"They're hardly legendary," I say.

"Oh, you were always so modest, Reagan. They are legendary. You need to learn how to take a compliment," Ella says.

And you need to learn how to give one.

"So, how's the baby?" Helen asks. "Do you have pictures?" She laughs at her own comment. "Of course you have pictures! What kind of mother doesn't have pictures of her firstborn child?"

Ella gets us seated on the sofa, then heads to the kitchen to get her mother a coffee. I scroll through my phone and show her some of my shots. Helen *oohs* and *aahs*, and we get through it without a sympathetic head tilt or a reference to how hard it all is. No mention about how nobody tells you what it's really like, having a baby. And I have hope that maybe, just maybe, she doesn't know about how much I've been struggling.

After a bit, Helen sighs. There's a faraway look in her eye. "I loved that phase," she says. "When they were so little and cuddly and helpless. It's nice to be needed, you know? Now that my grandkids are in school, well, it's different.

They have their own lives. That's why they're at my son's place this weekend with their cousins and not with us. We're old. Boring!"

"Oh, no," I say. "You look fantastic. A real glamma."

Helen fluffs her chestnut bob and waves off my comment. "You're too kind, Reagan. I tell you, becoming a grandmother was nothing like I'd imagined it would be. I mean that in a good way. It was so much more powerful. I'm sure your mother feels the same way. Is she involved?"

"Yes. Very." I roll my eyes and crack a smile.

"Oh, I know that look, Reagan! Ella would have said the same thing about me. We can't help but butt in. It's genetic. You just wait and see. Trust me, it's better that way. Your child will grow up surrounded by so much love. It's the best gift you can give your child. Not everyone is so lucky, to be loved unconditionally by so many people. Some children have nobody, and it's so..." Helen shakes her head and takes a minute, trying to compose herself.

Tears pool in her eyes as she purses her lips, deep in thought, it seems.

She excuses herself to use the restroom.

This day is getting weirder by the hour.

My mind flashes to Lanie. Is that what she means? Some children have nobody? Or am I reading too much into it? Lanie wasn't lucky, that's for sure.

Not in birth.

Even less so in death.

Ella comes out of the kitchen with Helen's coffee, and I inform her that her mother is in the bathroom. When Helen returns, she takes her coffee and says she needs to lie down for a few minutes in Ella's room.

"We need to get a move on the memorial service. The storm has intensified," Ella tells us. "And it's headed our way."

I see an out, and I take it. "Oh, wow. Well, I'd say let's do the service now, as soon as Brady and Josh get back. And then I think I'll get going back home after that."

"Oh, no, Reagan," Ella says. "It's coming from the southeast. Power has been knocked out in a bunch of towns from here to Albany. It's not safe to drive. You'll need to hunker down here for the night and ride it out."

Is that why I couldn't reach Matt and Danny?

A prickly sensation zaps me at the base of my skull. My legs feel like they might give out on me, but I fight to keep a calm look on my face. I don't want to fuel the notion that I'm unstable. "I need to try and call home," I say.

Brady walks in the door.

Ella updates Brady about the storm and the need to push up the timeline for the memorial service. "Did you happen to see Josh on your run?" Ella asks.

"Nope," he says.

"He said he was going out for a short run," Ella tells Brady. "There's really only one path that's suitable for jogging. I'm surprised you didn't pass him."

Brady shrugs. "He might be off the grid, knowing him. He likes trail runs. Call him, I guess."

Ella opens her screen and punches his number on her phone. "It went to voicemail," she says. "But that's not unusual. The coverage is so spotty here."

"He's probably out of range," Ted offers. "It's touch and go with the service, in the cabin and out in the woods."

"Did it ring first?" I ask.

"Yes," she says.

"Then he's not out of range," I point out.

Ella shrugs. "Well, let's get our things together and prepare to head out as soon as my father gets back from the store. I'm sure Josh will be back soon. And if he's not, we'll just have to do it without him. He probably went for that hike after all, knowing him."

But a chill runs up my spine. Josh is a little self-absorbed, sure. Out of all of us, he's the most likely to blow off Lanie's service and do what he wants. Something isn't sitting right with me, though. This is odd. He knows we were leaving soon. He liked Lanie. Much more than I knew. He maybe even loved her, which I have to admit, paints his break-up with me in a different light. If he dumped me because he really loved her and not me, well, I suppose that's better than simply wanting some variety.

Could he really be that self-absorbed, to go for a hike instead of memorializing the woman he claims to have loved?

Or is history repeating itself?

Will we find another twisted body before this weekend is over?

And I wish I'd never set foot in this cabin again.

THIRTEEN
ELLA

As Ella prepares to head out to the ravine for the memorial service, her mind flashes to the unfortunate turn of events ten years earlier. She remembers clearly the fear that mushroomed into full-blown panic when Lanie could not be found that morning. Well, it's a bit more than simply remembering it. It's as if she's reliving it.

A tightness in the chest.

A feeling of dread.

She takes a deep breath and wills herself to calm down.

Ted was the first to notice that Lanie was missing. Ella was still sleeping off the evening festivities in the master bedroom.

"Ella?" Ted said, pulling the covers off of her head, letting the morning light in under the covers.

She squinted as the rays pierced her eyes. "What?"

"We can't find Lanie. She's not in the cabin."

All of them except Josh had planned to stay in the cabin

that night. Josh brought a tent. Things had gotten out of hand the night before, she recalled. Reagan almost fell into the fire. The local guys were out of control. She should have shut the party down. Truthfully, though, she was a little afraid of those townies herself, and she couldn't very well call the cops. She hadn't taken any molly, but she was high, and pot was illegal back then.

"She's probably in Josh's tent," Ella said.

Sometimes that happened. Random hookups. And Lanie and Josh had history. She'd seen them kiss. It made the most sense, so she suggested it. Ted left to see if he could locate Lanie in Josh's tent.

Of course, when they found Josh, he was alone and fast asleep. He said that Lanie had made it clear she had no interest in hooking up with him that night, or ever. Then Lanie told him she was going to the cabin to use the bathroom.

But about ten minutes later, Josh said he saw her heading for the woods. He figured the bathroom line was too long and she couldn't wait; he didn't see her again after that. They all told the cops that Lanie was drunk, to make a stumble into the ravine seem more plausible, which Ella knows was a lie. Lanie wasn't wasted. Reagan was wasted, along with most everyone else, except Ella. Ella was somewhere between tipsy and sober.

But that was their story, ten years ago.

Lanie went into the woods to pee.

She was wasted.

She stumbled and fell down into the ravine.

She snapped her neck and died.

That's their story now.

And if anyone tries to mess with it, there's going to be trouble.

ELLA COMES out of the bedroom. Everyone except Josh is waiting for her. Ted and her parents hold the bouquets of flowers they plan to place at the site where her body was found, and her mother passes one to her. They are lovely. All white. Lilies and roses with baby's breath peppered in, and a sprinkle of greenery that adds a splash of color.

Ella grips the paper with the words she'll read in her other hand. Her sweaty palms dampen it a little, and the ink starts to run. She hopes she doesn't choke on the words. All she wants now is to get this out of the way. Move on with her life. And never see these people again.

"Josh isn't back yet?" she says.

"Nope," Ted replies. "Just like him. He's so selfish. I don't think he came here to pay tribute to Lanie. He's probably still pissed about the fact that she turned him down ten years ago."

Ella protests, but it's only for show. "Oh, come on, Ted. He's not that bad."

"Isn't he?" Brady says. "I'd be fine if I never saw Josh Tanner again in my life."

"Well, let's hope that doesn't happen," Reagan says. "We're here for Lanie, so let's be civilized about this."

Ella's mother jumps in. "Yes, Reagan's right. Let's stop this negativity and think positive. For Lanie, okay? She was like a second daughter to me. We need to keep the focus on her. That's why we're here. We don't need any more animosity between any of you."

After a bit of grandstanding about Lanie and how sad they all are, they head out to the ravine for the service. There's a massive wave of emotion welling up inside her, but Ella steels herself and carries on.

FOURTEEN
REAGAN

It's not easy to get down to the ravine. The stream dried up eons ago so there's no rushing water to worry about, but rainwater trapped under the foliage forms a slippery layer of mud that sometimes hides under fallen leaves, making it dangerous.

A steep switchback path is the quickest way down, but Helen says she doesn't want to risk twisting her ankle. She's wearing a sensible walking shoe. I can't tell what brand. It's not suitable for muddy, rocky terrain, she claims. She asks me to hold her bouquet until we get to the bottom.

Because of this, we need to go around the mountain the longer way and prolong the agony. Everyone is eerily quiet, and all I can hear is the crunch of leaves and the occasional sucking sound when one of us hits a muddy patch of ground.

Towering trees block the sun, and moisture is trapped inside the forest. It smells dank, like rotting leaves and earthworms. The absence of birds chirping and a stillness in the air reminds us of the impending storm, and I wish I could leave directly after the service. Maybe I still can. Even if I don't make it home, I'd prefer to take my chances in the storm and stay at a hotel rather than sleep another night in that cabin with these people.

Helen seems particularly distressed. She mumbled something about Lanie being like a second daughter to her when we were in the cabin. It seems as if they were closer than I thought. Ella's father is hard to read. Stoic, maybe? Or is he still concerned about a possible criminal investigation or lawsuit? As I said, they got lucky in Lanie's case. If that had been me, my parents would have sued the pants off them. Perhaps he's angry at Ella for getting them into this position in the first place. They've hardly said a word to each other.

And what about Josh? Where is he? Would he really stay away this long, just out of spite? That seems harsh, even for him. Maybe he twisted an ankle or broke a leg and needs our help. I'm surprised at Brady's reaction, too. He's a doctor. Even though Josh is an asshole, didn't he take that Hippocratic Oath? He should be the first one out there looking for him, making sure that he's not injured.

But then I think about the look on Brady's face when Josh made that crack and kept calling him Brainy. It was a look I'd never seen before. Not hot anger. More like a cold stare, which might be even worse.

And what about Ella and Josh in the kitchen this morning? Something was up with those two. What if they're having an affair? What if Ted found out? He was eager to brush Josh's absence off to selfishness. There's certainly no shortage of people who despise Josh Tanner, myself included. Would one of them actually harm him, though? I find that hard to believe. But then, look what happened to Lanie.

Finally, we get to the spot where we found Lanie ten years ago. All thoughts of Josh leave my mind, and a chill permeates my bones as soon as we stop moving. I hand Helen the bouquet and she nods me a thanks. The rain is coming, you can smell it, and the temperature has dropped. A moist mist hangs in the air, seeping in through my pores.

The six of us form a circle around the spot where we found her. I remember the last time I was here like it was yesterday. Looking down from the ridge and seeing Lanie lying there, all twisted and broken. I stayed up top with Ted and Ella. Brady and Josh hurried down the switchback trail.

It was Brady who confirmed that she was dead. Lanie's neck had been snapped in the fall. He thought that she'd probably died instantly, he told us on the walk back to the house, which comforted us a little. Better than the thought of her lying there all night, suffering.

None of us had phone service at the spot where we were, so we didn't call for help. But when we got near the cabin, Josh started to call 911, and that's when Ella freaked out. She pointed out that Lanie was already dead. There was nothing we could do for her anyway. She insisted we clean up the evidence before we called them. I remember thinking that it was awfully callous of her at the time, but we were young and selfish and had our whole lives ahead of us.

Unlike Lanie.

Ella takes a deep breath and hands her bouquet to Ted. She straightens out the paper in her hand. Then she looks up at all of us, seemingly to get our approval that she should begin. This isn't a formal service. There aren't any rules. We're all winging it here.

Her eyes lock on to mine.

I shrug.

She begins.

"Lanie," she says.

Then, to my utter shock, Ella chokes up. She starts to sob, and Ted pulls her in for a hug.

"Take your time, honey," her mother says.

"I'm sorry. I'm just..."

I say nothing, too shocked by her outpouring of emotion to feel any kind of ripple effect. It seemed to me, earlier on, as if this was all for show. Like Ella didn't care that much about Lanie and her death. Perhaps I was wrong. Looking at the faces of the others, I'm trying to gauge their reactions. Tears pool in Helen's eyes. Brady and Ella's father are stone-faced. Ted's look I can only describe as pained.

Then Ella clears her throat and starts again, reading from the paper in her hand. Her words are unremarkable. She talks about a life cut way too short. How we miss her terribly, which is kind of an exaggeration. If she'd lived, chances are none of us would be in touch at all.

She ends with a little prayer.

We're all silent for a few moments, and I see Lanie in my mind's eye, a smile on her face during better days. She was fun and exciting, and I miss her. I hadn't realized how much until right now, and I wonder if she knew that Josh was in love with her.

Ella takes one of the bouquets from her husband, bends down, and places it on the ground. Ted and her mother follow suit.

There's not much to say after that.

We start to head out.

But Ella turns around once more.

She looks to the memorial site, and my gaze goes with her.

The white flowers remind me of death now, like a person with the blood drained out of them. Lilies and roses and tiny baby's breath buds left there to rot on the moist patch of earth.

"Sorry, Lanie," she says.

Sorry for what?

FIFTEEN
REAGAN

When we get back to the cabin, the first thing we notice is that Josh is not back yet. We've been gone over an hour. Why isn't he back? He should be back by now, which we all point out in various ways, with different levels of urgency to our observations.

Brady appears calm, or maybe that's just his affect. "He probably went for that hike," Brady says.

Ella seems more distraught than I would have imagined she'd be, but she's not saying much. It's her expression. She's gone pale. There must be something going on between the two of them.

The rest of us are concerned, rather than panicked.

We take turns using the restroom while we weigh our options.

"That storm is coming," I remind everyone. "If we want to look for Josh, we need to do it soon."

"Maybe he came back and we weren't here, and then he

went out to the site to try and catch up with us," Helen offers.

"We would have seen him," Ella says.

"Not if he went the short way down to the ravine," Ted says.

"I'll check his room," Ella says. "If he came back from a run, he would probably have changed clothes before coming to the service."

Ella comes out of Josh's bedroom, shaking her head. "Looks like his stuff is in the same place. I don't think he's been back here."

"Okay," Brady says. "Ted and I can go out and look for him. How much time until the storm hits?" he asks.

Ella heads over near the kitchen window, where the cell reception is better, to check the weather updates. A ping rings out from her phone. She looks down at the screen and her face lights up. "It's him! He says he's fine."

Then she clutches at her chest and steadies herself by putting her other hand on the kitchen counter.

"Oh, that's great," I say.

Ella continues. "He said he needed some time alone. And that he's sorry. He'll be back soon."

"Well, that's a relief," Helen says.

"Absolutely," Ella's father adds. "And I'm afraid we need to get a move on if we're going to beat the storm. It's midday already. You should have enough batteries for those flashlights if you lose power tonight. Are you sure you have enough supplies to see you through for a few days? It shouldn't be that bad, but you never know."

"Yes, Dad," Ella says. "We'll be fine."

As we start to say our goodbyes, Ella's father addresses

us. His look is stern but not menacing. "I trust you can all behave yourselves this weekend. We don't need a repeat of ten years ago. Are we all clear on that?"

He stops to look each and every one of us in the eye, and I now see why they came here. They're checking up on us, and I can't say I blame them.

With subtle nods of our heads, we all confirm that we've gotten the message, loud and clear. Ella and Ted head out with her parents, leaving Brady and me alone in the cabin.

"What do you make of all this?" I ask Brady, now that I've got him alone. "Didn't Ella seem a little emotional? About Josh?"

"I didn't notice anything," he says.

"Really? She looked like she had to steady herself on the counter when she got that text. Like she was so overcome with emotion, she almost needed to sit down. Don't you find that a little odd?"

"What are you getting at, Reagan?"

I sigh, hoping this isn't a big mistake. Brady doesn't like gossip, and I can't afford to alienate my only ally. But I don't have much choice, now that I've started. I proceed to tell him about what I saw this morning, being careful not to sound salacious. And what I saw ten years ago—Josh and Ella huddled together in some kind of intense conversation.

"Something's up with the two of them, Brady. I'm telling you. Those aren't two people who haven't seen each other in over a decade. I'm not saying it's an affair or anything. But what if it has something to do with what happened to Lanie?"

"I think you're letting your imagination get the better of you, Reagan. Josh is fine. He said so in the text. Maybe he liked Lanie more than we thought, and he needed some time to process it."

That's an insightful observation, and I tell him so.

He shrugs. "Well, he did try to hit on her that night. We know that much. And she blew him off. He acts like he doesn't care that much about women, but I always got the feeling that he liked Lanie more than he let on."

Did he like her enough to push her down into a ravine when she rejected him?

Is he staying away out of guilt?

But of course, I don't say this to Brady.

"Wow." I nod. "I never looked at it that way before. Good point, Brady. But then, he broke up with her, so what did he expect?"

I know that Josh told me that Lanie broke up with him, but I'm not sure if I believe him. Lanie's not around to challenge his claim, so I'm feeling out Brady.

"Oh, no. That's not true. Lanie broke up with him. Josh told me so himself. It's the only time Josh got real with me, so it's not something I'd forget. He was pretty broken up about it."

Widening my eyes, I feign surprise. "Are you sure? That's not what Lanie told me. She said Josh dumped her too."

Brady shrugs. "Maybe she was trying to make you feel better," he says.

I guess it's true then, and I'm the only one who didn't know the truth. And if so, it was kind of Lanie to try and spare my feelings. But I wonder if there could be some other reason she rejected Josh that night. Like maybe she was seeing someone else, and didn't want anyone to know about it.

Could Lanie have made a play for Ted?

There was a lot of tension between Ella and Lanie the weekend she died. And Ella's mother said that Lanie was like a second daughter to her. Ella said she was sorry. Could Ella have been jealous enough of Lanie to have...

"What's wrong, Reagan? You look upset. Did that bother you? The thought of Lanie with Josh?"

"No." I wave off his comment. "Not in the slightest. I was thinking it through, that's all."

And then I explain to Brady that, although I believe him when he says I was angry at Lanie that night, I tell him that I don't think it was because of Josh. I go on to recount my recollection of Josh and Ella, and how my first thoughts were about Ted and how unfair that would be to him. And my second thought was that I wanted to leave and go back to Matt.

"Just like now," I add. "I miss Matt and Danny. I want to go home." I'm not sure if he believes me, but I don't care. It's true, and he can think what he wants.

"Me too," he says. "I'd leave now if it weren't for the storm."

"Just our luck. I mean, it's not winter. Who would have thought we'd get stuck here in late September? Seems like the least risky time of year in terms of weather."

Brady shrugs. "So, you weren't mad at Lanie about Josh. Does that mean you were mad at her about something else?"

I let out a breath, part of me wanting to keep this inside, but a bigger part of me needing to get it out in the open. "Maybe," I say. "I think she may have told me something."

"Like what?"

"Honestly, I don't remember. My memory is coming back in chunks, and they're out of order. I can't piece it together yet. But, Brady. I want to ask you a question. And I need you to tell me the truth."

"What, Reagan?"

"Do you believe that Lanie's death was an accident?" I ask.

"Look, if I were you, I'd leave that genie in the bottle. You claim you saw a lot of things that night, but you were wasted. And on drugs. You say you heard a scream that night, which none of us heard. You say you saw some biker guy hit on Lanie, which none of us saw. And if anyone were to go digging into what happened to Lanie ten years ago, I'd need to tell the truth. And the truth is, you were the only person I saw who was angry at Lanie Martin the night she died. So, do you still want me to answer that question?"

My stomach sinks, and I find myself at a loss for words.

"That's what I thought. I'm going for a walk. I need some time alone."

With that, Brady turns on his heel and heads out the front door.

SIXTEEN
REAGAN

Standing by the kitchen window, I finally manage to get Matt on the phone. The bands of rain have arrived and there's a steady pattering outside. Not a downpour yet, but it's headed our way, that's for certain. My husband assures me that he and Danny are fine and tells me that the rain has let up there. It was very heavy overnight and some water seeped into the garage, damaging some of the paper products that were stored there, but otherwise all is well. The power went out for a few hours but it's back now, he says.

I hear rain in the background, I think. "It sounds like it's starting up again," I say.

"No, it's just the connection. We're fine," Matt says.

This is a big relief for me. *They're fine.* Not everyone was so lucky, he says. We aren't in a flood zone, but Matt reports that some of the neighborhoods near streams and waterways sustained a lot more damage. As an insurance guy, he's got his hands full, and he's eager for me to get home. I fill him in on the ceremony, and that we've pretty much put that behind us, so there's not much reason for me to be here any longer.

"I want to come home now," I say.

"It's not safe to drive, Reagan."

"It might not be safe to stay here either."

"The cabin will be fine. You're not near a stream, as I recall."

"That's not what I meant. Josh is missing. Ella is acting weird. Did you tell her I tried to kill myself?" I had planned to wait until I saw him to bring that up, but it slipped out.

"What? No," Matt says. "And what do you mean Josh is missing?"

And then my bars disappear, cutting me off from civilization.

Stranding me, in all ways possible.

A feeling of dread squeezes my insides like a vise.

Ted and Ella come out from their bedroom.

"We need to store some water," Ted says to Ella. "Just in case the pumps fail."

She nods and heads to the kitchen.

Brady is out for his walk. Josh is still not back yet, and if we don't have cell service, he won't be able to communicate with us. It's been over an hour since he sent that text stating that he needed some time alone. Shouldn't he be back by now?

And now I'm the only one here.

Alone with Ted and Ella.

And Then There Were None.

Matt and I watched a recent adaption of Agatha Christie's classic novel a few weeks ago, a British mini-series from a few years back, and right now, I feel as if I'm living it.

The gaslighted protagonist who doesn't know her own mind.

But I'm not going to let myself become unhinged. That seemed to be her downfall. I'm determined to appear calm, although I'm trembling inside.

Then a strange thought occurs to me as I recall my recent conversation with Matt. The hairs on the back of my neck stand up. Once again, I question myself and what I think I heard him say, after I told him that I didn't feel safe staying here.

You'll be fine.

The cabin's not near a stream, as I recall.

Because Matt's never been to Ella's camp, as far as I know. Why would he say something like that? Did I describe it to him and he's recalling my description? But then why wouldn't he say *from what you told me*? Has he been here himself, and I didn't know about it?

But when?

And why?

This is crazy, I tell myself.

I'm going to drive myself insane.

Stop, Reagan.

Get a grip.

Ted snaps me out of my stupor.

"Reagan," Ted says. "Did you hear me? I said, are you hungry? We're going to make some lunch."

Lunch?

How can we think about food at a time like this?

But I play along. "Sure."

I'll make myself eat. I need to keep up my strength, and they can't know that I'm afraid of them.

"I finally got hold of Matt," I say. "They're fine. Just a bit of water seepage in the garage, but he said other areas were hit pretty hard. Neighborhoods near streams and rivers, because they flooded. He's got his hands full already with all the clients calling to file claims."

Ted tries to put me at ease. "I'm sure that's a relief for you. We'll be fine here at the cabin. We're not close to any waterways. But the road down might become impassable. That's what happened with Hurricane Beryl a few years back. It took a day or two before Ella's parents could come check on the cabin."

Impassable, soon.
But the road is passable now?
Perhaps I should leave.

As soon as the thought enters my mind, sheets of rain start to pummel the cabin. The storm is closing down on us. It goes from pitter-patter to a roaring sound in a matter of minutes. If I didn't know better, I'd think it was a wildfire.

Where the hell is Brady?

Why would he stay out this long?

I speak up about it, and Ella echoes my concerns.

"Maybe I should go look for him," Ted offers.

"No! Stay here with me, Ted. It's not safe outside. And we need to finish preparing for the storm. It's here already. We're running out of time."

Ella seems totally freaked out by the thought of Ted leaving. It's not *that* bad out yet. Is she afraid to be here alone with me? Does she not trust me? Does she not trust herself?

"Okay, calm down, Ella. I'll stay here," Ted says.

"I've filled up the bathtub," she says. "Do you think that will be enough water, with what we have in the fridge? I filled all of our containers and stored them in the fridge, and I've refilled the ice trays twice."

"Yeah," Ted says. "The storm's moving fast, which means less flooding. We rarely ever lose water. We'll probably lose electricity at some point, but we can make it one night. It won't be that bad. Don't worry. Let's get some food in our systems. The last thing we need is a bunch of hangry people stranded together in a cabin."

Ted smiles.

Ella and I don't.

He sets out some sandwich food on a platter.

Bread. Turkey. Ham. Cheese. Condiments.

I wonder how much food we actually have, and how long we might be stuck here. A sinking feeling settles in my stomach as I consider how tense that could get. We start to fix our sandwiches as Brady comes bursting through the door.

He shakes his head. Water droplets fly off his dripping wet hair and his shoes slosh as he walks. He's positively drenched.

"I looked for Josh. There's no sign of him," Brady says. "Maybe we should call the police."

This makes me feel better, that someone here has a sense of responsibility about this. Josh may be a jackass, but still. He's our friend. At least, he was our friend. He's a human being, in any case. We can't just write him off in a storm like this.

Ella agrees, and tries to get some bars on her phone, standing in the spot that usually offers a few bars of service, allowing a call to get through. "The cell tower must have gotten knocked out. I have nothing," she says.

"I can try to drive into town," Brady says. "Let me go change first."

No, I almost cry out. I don't want to be stuck here with Ella and Ted.

"No," Ted says. "I'll go. I know the roads better than you do. I can check with some of the neighbors. Maybe one of them has a landline."

That makes me feel better. If Ted and Ella are up to something, it'll be two on one. Brady and I are on the same team, I think.

But then I remember what he said.

You're the only one I saw who was mad at Lanie that night.

And Ella told Brady I tried to kill myself.

I want to get out of here, but I can't. So, I'll opt for the next best thing. After forcing down half a sandwich, I excuse myself. "My stomach is bothering me," I say. "I'm going to lie down in my room."

When I close the bedroom door behind me, I can't help but notice there's no lock on the door. I look around for something I could use to barricade it shut.

And I wonder if I'm starting to lose it.

DRIFTING.

Floating.

Gyrating to the music.

A crackling noise.

Something is loud now.

Very loud.

Rapid. A staccato-sound.

A punch to the gut startles me.

My heart races.

Pa-pa-pa-pa-pa-pa.

Are we being ambushed?

Is it gunfire?

My eyes flutter open and I see that I'm in bed. I must have drifted off.

The sound from my dream fills my ears. It does sound a little like gunfire. Water pummels the rustic cabin, hitting the metal gutters along with the rest of the structure, and as solid as it is, suddenly it seems flimsy and inadequate against the raw power of nature.

Something is hovering on the edge of my consciousness, though.

Something about that night ten years ago, when I was lying in this same bed.

It's something about Lanie. But what was it?

I close my eyes and try to sink back into it. I start to drift off again, images from then and now merging in my mind, set to the backdrop of the storm that's now barreling down on us, no doubt making the roads impassable.

The wind makes a whistling sound that reminds me of being inside a haunted house on Halloween. I used to love that holiday as a kid, and I can only hope I get out of here in one piece, in time for Danny's first one, just a month from now.

Recalling what my therapist said about how memories return, I try to relax and let my mind go.

And then it comes.

In one big bolt of lightning.

A realization flashes in my mind's eye, as if I'd always known it.

Lanie was pregnant.

Except, that's all I remember.

I don't remember how I know this.

No image in my mind exists of her telling me about it.

I don't remember whose baby it was, or if I even knew that at the time.

I also remember being annoyed with her, but I'm not sure I was upset about this. Why would I be mad and not supportive? Unless it was Josh's baby? Was I that confused, that I thought the two of them betrayed me, and that I was still with him? But then why did she blow him off that night? And why did I not care about seeing Josh and Ella together?

None of this makes any sense in terms of that night, but at least I have an explanation for why this all came up for me again after I gave birth. Because Lanie wasn't the only person who died that night, and I'm sure I was reminded of that when I held my newborn in my arms and nurtured him through his first few weeks of life. That's about the time I started thinking about her again.

Yes, that part makes sense. Lanie was pregnant. An innocent little baby was inside of her. The birth of Danny triggered that for me. And then another more terrible thought occurs to me.

Was Lanie upset enough to have...

No. It's impossible, I tell myself.

But I know that it's not. The hormones wreak havoc on your body and your mind. Rethinking the events from a new perspective, I have to admit it adds up. Was she distraught? Did she take her own life? It's more believable than Lanie stumbling off a cliff, and probably more believable than a murder.

Unless the father was someone it shouldn't have been.

My mind flashes to Ella. Something is at the edge of my consciousness about Ella and that night. Was Ella with us when Lanie told me about the baby? Could Ted have been the father of her child? Is that why Ella was so eager to close the lid on it and not have the police do an autopsy?

But I have no memory of Lanie telling me she was pregnant. So how do I know this? Did Ella tell me? Ella was always a bit jealous of Lanie. But then I'm the one who called Lanie a bitch. Could I have been messed up enough to think that Lanie betrayed me? Could I have been messed up enough to...

No. There's no way. I'm not a murderer. I would never do something like that. Murder is the least likely explanation, in general. What are the chances of that? Probably very slim. And who would go that far just to keep Lanie's pregnancy a secret?

Another thought occurs to me. If Lanie was pregnant, she would not likely have been drinking, making an accident the least likely explanation.

I'm left with suicide or murder.

And in either case, one thing seems clear: the father was someone it shouldn't have been.

Who were you sleeping with, Lanie?

Who was the father of your child?

And could that have pushed you over the edge?

THEN

SEVENTEEN
REAGAN

Someone lit the firepit, I see, as I come out of the cabin after using the bathroom. I wonder where Ella went.

That was so weird. Ella was on the phone when I entered the cabin, and it seemed like she didn't want me to hear her. Who was she talking to, I wonder? Everyone she knows is here, except maybe her parents? Maybe they called to check up on us? Yes, that makes sense.

But who are all these people I don't recognize?

I hang back a bit and take a deep breath, scanning the area for one of my close friends, but I don't see any of them. Maybe I shouldn't have come here this weekend.

Matt and I had a fight before I left. A really big fight. He didn't want me to come up to the camp. I told him that he was more than welcome to join us. Assured him that everyone wanted him here, which was mostly a lie. Matt's a bit of a killjoy, truth be told. The only one who likes having him around is Brainy, because Brainy doesn't party much anymore and he probably likes having someone around who can carry on a conversation as the night wears on.

Actually, all six of us have mellowed over the years, but as Matt feared, this is going to be a raging, post-graduation blowout. The night is young, and already, people are stumbling around, me included.

And who can blame us?

Where's the harm?

It's not like we're out clubbing and one of us will get behind the wheel and kill someone. We're all up at the camp. It's safe. We don't have to risk getting into a car with a stranger or getting mugged in the city or sexually assaulted by some creep at a bar who follows us home.

We're in the middle of nowhere!

I stretch my arms up to the sky and smile.

The stars poke through the dark night sky.

I wave at them.

Wait?

Did I say that out loud?

I'm drunk already.

Maybe I should eat something.

Oh, who cares?

I deserve a night like this.

I've been so good this year. I've been taking my medication. Going to a therapist, although I don't think it's helping. She's constantly telling me that I need to *love myself*.

What the hell does that even mean?

With the medication I'm on, I'm not supposed to drink a lot. But even my psychiatrist says I can have one or two—which probably means three or four. She doesn't want to get sued, I'm sure, so I figure I can tack on a little more.

I just graduated college for Christ's sake.

Ha. I sound like my mother. She says that a lot.

For Christ's sake, Reagan.

What's gotten into you?

That's what she'd say if she were here—or worse.

I'm pacing myself, Mom. I'm not an idiot. I'll be fine.

I only took a half of a Zoloft, so I'm sure I'll be okay.

It's one last weekend.

One last weekend of abandon.

Then I'll be a good girl.

Forever.

I promise, I say, crossing my heart and smiling at my imaginary mother.

As I make my way to the firepit, some girl I've never seen before offers me a shot.

I down it.

I know. I know.

Bad Reagan.

Then I spot Lanie and start to walk over toward her. She's not smiling. I wonder what's up. This night is supposed to be fun, but she's not having any. That's clear. Her arms are crossed over her body, like she's hugging herself. Lanie looks over at Ella, and I stop to watch this for a minute or so.

Something seems off about Lanie, but I can't put my finger on what it is. Ella's blonde hair is blowing in the wind. She's smiling as she brushes it back from her face, talking to a couple I've never met before. They look about thirty or so. Local granolas.

Ted's next to Ella. She places a hand on Ted's forearm and he mutters something to her.

Ella turns her head and spots Lanie looking in her direction.

The two of them lock eyes.

Lanie turns away first.

I start to walk over toward them to see what's going on, because something is obviously going on between the two of them, but then I stumble.

Whoa.

I feel so...

Some guy grabs my arm. "Are you okay?" he asks.

I turn to him.

He looks old. Like in his thirties, maybe. A biker? His meaty arms poke through a sleeveless leather vest. His forearm sports a tattoo of a snake curling around a cross. He's got straggly dirty blond hair that's too long for this era.

He reminds me of a snake, come to think of it. So, I hiss at him.

Snake man flashes me a smile and sticks his tongue out. "I like feisty chicks," he says. His twisted teeth are a nasty shade of pale yellow.

Oh, why did I do that?

He's so getting the wrong idea.

He pulls me toward him and tries to kiss me.

I turn my head to the side just in time, but I still feel his slimy tongue on my cheek.

Oh God, he's so gross!

I try to pull away, but he's holding my arm.

"Let go of me," I say. "I have a boyfriend. He's right..."

I turn my head and look around. "Here."

Grabbing Josh by the arm as he's walking by, I spin

around and plant a kiss on him. I realize that I'm pretty drunk already. I haven't had all that much to drink, but I remember something about the medication making the alcohol more powerful. The shot was a bad idea, and I hardly ate anything today.

Josh shoves me away from him.

"What the fuck is wrong with you, Reagan? We've been over for years." He scoffs, looking at me with disgust. "You're pathetic."

I try to explain about the biker guy, but he's nowhere to be found.

Josh doesn't believe me. "Nice try, Reagan," he says. "A biker guy. Yeah, right. Don't worry, I won't tell Matt. It'll be our little secret."

What a douchebag he's being.

I feel like an idiot now.

It's so embarrassing.

But then why am I letting him get to me? I'm with Matt now. But Josh's rejection still stings, I'm sorry to admit. I'm his friend. Why doesn't he believe me? Does he think I somehow wanted to kiss him and that was just an excuse? Maybe I did, a little. I'm so confused.

Then my stomach sinks. What if someone saw me try to kiss Josh and they tell Matt? What will everyone think of me? What if Matt finds out?

Oh, the hell with it, I decide.

At least it worked.

The biker guy left.

Screw all of them, Matt included.

He could have come here with me. It's one weekend. He could be here, protecting me from creeps like that biker guy.

But he's not here.
So the hell with him.
Maybe he's not the one, after all.
And if this is my last hurrah, I'm going to make it count.
I reach into my pocket and grab a molly.
And pop it into my mouth.

EIGHTEEN
REAGAN

My mind is a maze of confusion—and I like it.

Slipping in and out of the growing crowd, I look for someone I know. But I don't see my friends. The fire is much bigger now. There must be fifty or more partiers, most of them from here, but some from college. The music is getting louder. People are starting to dance. I hear random shrieks and laughter and the crackling of the fire. A smoky haze fills my nostrils and lingers in the air.

I need to explain to Josh what happened. That I was trying to get away from snake man. I wasn't really trying to kiss him. Where are my friends? I need to find my friends. I have to explain it to them. Or maybe I can make some new ones.

Old friends.
New friends.
Who cares?
It's all good!
Cause I feel sooooo grrreat!

The music is louder now.

It seeps into my pores, like I'm one with it.

There's the girl with the shots. Maybe I can get another one.

"Hey, what's your name again?" I ask.

"Jeanine," she says.

"Oh, yeah," I say, although I don't think I ever knew her name.

I'm about to ask her for another shot. But then I see the biker guy, over near the fire. He grabs Lanie by the arm and spins her around. Maybe he thinks she's me. I need to help her. I leave my new friend Jeanine and push my way through the crowd, but I lose sight of Lanie in the chaos.

People are dancing now.

I start to swirl around to the music and close my eyes.

Wait.

What was I doing?

I remember I was doing something, but it doesn't seem important now.

But wasn't it important?

Lanie.

Right.

I was going to rescue Lanie.

Glancing around, I see Lanie's standing a few people away from me, and the biker guy is gone. She's safe. She's with Josh. Maybe he saved her.

Why wouldn't he do the same for me?

They are huddled close together.

I stop dancing and walk over to them.

Neither of them is happy to see me.

"We're in the middle of something, Reagan," Josh says, a look of scorn on his face.

What's wrong with him?
Why is he looking at me that way?

"You have to be careful, Lanie," I say. "He's creepy. Stay away from him."

"You're wasted, Reagan," Lanie says. "Please. Leave us alone."

"I'm just trying to help. He tried to kiss me."

"What the fuck are you talking about, Reagan? You tried to kiss me," Josh says.

"Not you. The snake man," I say.

Lanie shakes her head. "You're embarrassing yourself, Reagan. Go inside and lie down," Lanie says.

Why are they being so mean to me?
I'm trying to help.

"Well, fuck you both then," I say.

And I walk away.

BRAINY'S STANDING ALONE near the edge of the yard. I walk over to him. "Hey," I say. "Wanna dance?" I grab his hand and try to pull him, but he doesn't budge.

"I'm not much of a dancer," he says, stumbling forward a bit as I yank on him.

"Oh, c'mon! It'll be fun!" Taking his hand, I try to twirl him around.

He pulls away. "You're wasted, Reagan," he says.

We watch Lanie and Josh stroll away from the crowd toward the woods. Josh puts his arm around her shoulder.

"She's such a bitch," I say to Brainy.

He narrows his eyes on me. "Take it easy, Reagan."

The fire is getting bigger and bigger. The flames dance around. I want to be one with them. I leave Brainy and head to the firepit.

Closing my eyes, I dance and twirl.

I'm getting dizzy, but it's fun.

Nirvana.

So fitting. This feels like nirvana.

A few minutes later, I hear a scream.

At least I think it was a scream.

Lanie went into the woods.

Who was she with?

Maybe the biker guy got her?

I grab the person next to me.

"Did you hear that?" I ask.

"Hear what?" the girl yells over the music.

"Never mind," I say.

Maybe it was my scream.

Maybe I'm losing my mind.

One last night.

And then I'll be a good girl.

NINETEEN
ELLA

Things are getting out of control, Ella realizes. She's trying to hold it together, but she knows this is bad. Scanning the area, it looks like they are headed for trouble. A dozen or so biker guys and chicks mix with older couples, granola types, and stoners who live in the area. She and her friends are outnumbered. Ella hadn't expected so many locals to come.

There's a neighbor girl from a cabin nearby, about five years older than them, who still lives with her parents and works as a bartender at a local restaurant. Jeanine is her name. Ella invited her because she thought it would make her less likely to call the cops on them.

Jeanine's parents are away this weekend, she said. Most of the other cabins this far up are seasonal, and used mostly in the ski season. Most of the locals live closer to the city center. She must've told the whole town about it, and she brought a ton of hard liquor with her, which is making this so much worse. She's not the brightest bulb on the porch. Ella had opted for keg beer, figuring that there's only so plastered you can get on beer, since it makes you so full. Ella looks around for Jeanine, thinking that maybe she can get her to calm the rest of them down. She thinks about calling the cops herself, but she's high, and that would be bad. The only thing she can think of is to try and get rid of some of the hard liquor. Let people drink beer from the kegs, which should be running dry soon anyway. If the alcohol runs out, people will leave. Maybe they'll go over to Jeanine's place.

So, she sneaks around the grounds, grabbing bottles of Jack Daniels or Stoli or whatever she can snatch without people seeing her. Then she pours out the contents, letting the liquid seep into the hungry earth, hoping that she can get this crowd sobered up enough so that nobody drives drunk. Her parents could get sued if anything happens. And maybe she could too. She's over eighteen. This could derail her whole life.

Ella's so consumed with fear about what might happen that, for a time, she forgot about the disastrous situation with Lanie. But when she comes around the corner from the back of the house where she'd been dumping out the booze, Ella spots Lanie. It all comes racing back to her. Lanie is facing in Ella's direction, talking to a guy whose back is to Ella, off to the far end of the front yard near the start of the woods. The two of them are standing close together.

Who is she talking to?

Is that Josh?

Ella sees the guy brush back Lanie's auburn hair.

He caresses her face and pulls her in for a kiss. She's pretty sure it's Josh.

God, Lanie's such a slut.

Ella shakes her head and carries on, trying to figure out how to further damp down the ruckus and get this party to burn itself out.

Oh shit!

The firepit!

The fire is raging. Flames shoot higher and higher up toward the night sky. People throw more fuel on it as they laugh and dance. Cardboard boxes. Wastepaper. Twigs and logs and who knows what else. It smells bad, maybe even toxic, like they're burning plastic.

Then Ella spots Reagan, teetering on the edge of the flames, wasted out of her mind. Reagan's dancing and twirling around and she's going to fall in the firepit if someone doesn't do something.

Dashing over, Ella knows she won't make it in time. Thankfully, a long-haired local landscaper named Jerry who always smells like patchouli oil, grabs Reagan just as she starts to tip over into the fire. He pulls her out just in time, frantically brushing the embers off her hair and peacoat. By the time Ella gets there, Reagan is nearly passed out. But at least she's not on fire.

Ella turns off the music.

"This needs to stop! *Now!*" Ella screams out. "Everyone, get away from the fire. This party needs to calm the fuck down!"

They all seem to get the message.

Brainy joins her.

But where the hell is Ted?

"Take Reagan into the house and put her in the bedroom," Ella commands. "Turn her on her side," she says.

Brainy complies.

The mood has shifted at the camp now. It seems like the party might finally start to die down. People huddle in small groups. Some of them sit, and Ella breathes a small sigh of relief. She decides to leave the music off and let the fire burn itself out.

All the hard liquor is gone, and the kegs should run out soon. She sees Jeanine and gently suggests that perhaps she and her friends could take the party over to her place.

"Oh, hell no," she says. "My parents would kill me."

Maybe Jeanine's not as dumb as she looks.

Then Ella heads into the house and grabs the bags of chips she was saving for the six of them. She passes out the junk food, hoping the munchies will sober them up a little.

It seems to work. Ella watches as people pass around the bags and make short work of their contents, greedily stuffing their faces with handfuls of chips.

And she starts to think that maybe, just maybe, she'll get through this evening without ruining her entire life.

TWENTY
REAGAN

What am I doing in the bedroom?

Where is everyone?

There's a trash can next to the bed and a bottle of water on the dresser.

It feels as if I'm dreaming. My head hurts. I drink some water.

I need to sleep more. My head sinks into the pillow and I drift off again.

But then I hear voices. Is someone in the room with me? Or am I dreaming?

No, it's voices. Coming from outside. I open my eyes.

The voices are coming in through the bedroom window.

They are not happy voices.

Not happy voices at all.

I should get up and look, but I'm too tired.

It's Lanie and...someone.

At least I think it's Lanie?

Lanie and a man?

I listen carefully, shutting my eyes tight, unsure if this is a dream, a hallucination, or a real conversation.

The man's voice is forceful but hushed. "You can't do this," he says.

The voice is vaguely familiar.

Maybe? Or maybe not.

"You need to take care of it," he says.

"No. That's not how it's going to work. I'm having this baby whether you like it or not," Lanie says.

"Be reasonable, Lanie," he says.

"Let go of me," Lanie cries out.

I open my eyes. I'm not dreaming.

"Come back here," the man calls out.

I fight to pull myself out of the quagmire, but I'm so tired. I know I should look out the window and see what's happening. But I can't get up.

It's obvious they're gone.

My head is so heavy.

I surrender to the pillow.

THE SUDDEN URGE to pee rouses me. I have no idea what time it is.

I had a dream. A weird dream, about Lanie and a guy and a baby.

But what if it wasn't a dream?

I remember seeing Lanie looking upset earlier in the evening.

I remember a biker guy was bothering her.

Oh crap.

I remember trying to kiss Josh—and I'm pretty sure that wasn't a dream. I'll need to do some damage control on that, because it's sure to get back to Matt. I can't let that stuck-up jackass ruin the best thing that ever happened to me.

Ella's sitting in the living room with her head in her hands when I come out of the bedroom. She doesn't acknowledge me, so I continue to the bathroom.

When I come out of the bathroom, I address Ella. "Have you seen Lanie in here? I think I heard her outside my window, talking to some guy. This might sound crazy, but I thought she said something about being pregnant?"

Ella's brows rise.

She looks at me like I've lost my mind.

Fair enough.

"Go back to sleep, Reagan," Ella says. "You're still high as a kite."

So, I go back to my bedroom and plop down onto the soft mattress. But before I drift off, I vow that I'll never, ever, do anything like this again.

As long as I live.

TWENTY-ONE
ELLA

Ella squints as the morning light shines through the windowpane like a dagger piercing her eyes. She didn't drink as much as everyone else last night, but she had enough to feel it this morning, and she needs more sleep.

Ted has lifted up the bedsheet, and he's staring at her.

"Why are you bothering me?" Ella says.

"You need to get up," Ted says. "We can't find Lanie."

Ella's stomach lurches. It all comes racing back to her. The entire, sordid train wreck of an evening barrels into her dull, achy mind, making her stomach turn. She takes a deep breath and tries to remain calm. "What do you mean, you can't find her?"

"Reagan woke to use the bathroom and Lanie wasn't in the room with her. I was up, making coffee."

Right. Reagan and Lanie were supposed to be sharing the bunk bed room.

"Did you check the other bedroom?" Ella asks.

"Yeah. Brainy's sleeping in there. Alone."

Ella purses her lips. "I saw Lanie kissing Josh last night. Check his tent."

"Do you know where he pitched it?" Ted asks. "I looked around the yard and didn't see it anywhere."

"I think he was camping further into the woods, in the direction of the ravine," Ella says.

"I'll go take a look," Ted replies.

Ella gets up to face the day, recalling with crystal clarity what Reagan said to her when she came out of the bathroom. Ella can only hope that Reagan was so out of it, she won't remember the conversation at all. If she does, perhaps Ella can convince her it was all a dream. At least she didn't say anything to Ted about Lanie being pregnant this morning, so perhaps that secret will stay hidden in the recesses of Reagan's drugged-up, drunken mind.

When Ella enters the living room, the cabin is dead still. Reagan must be sleeping it off, which is a good thing. Ella needs time to process everything that happened. Grabbing a coffee, she sits on the sofa and takes a moment for herself.

And then she starts cleaning up the mess.

EVERYONE'S UP NOW, and panic is starting to set in. All five of them are in the yard, pacing around, trying to decide what to do next, and how big of a deal this is.

"I'm telling you, she was upset about something," Josh says to everyone. "And she wouldn't tell me what it was. Then she walked to the cabin to use the bathroom and I went to join the party. About ten minutes later, I saw her head to the woods. I figured she went to pee there because the line was too long inside. I didn't see her after that."

Ella is grateful that Josh didn't disclose to all of them what he found out last night from Lanie. According to Josh, Lanie told him what she was upset about, and Josh questioned Ella about it earlier this morning, when they first noticed she was missing. Lanie's car is still here, but Josh thought that, in light of what he found out, she may have left the camp with someone. Ella begged Josh to keep that information himself, for Lanie's sake. It was Lanie's news to tell, not Josh's.

"I'll keep it to myself. But for her, not for you," Josh replied. "Because you're right. I made her that promise, that I wouldn't tell anyone. You don't count, because she told me that she told you about it, given the situation."

"And you can see why you have to keep it quiet. Please, Josh. Promise me."

But every time Josh opens his mouth, Ella holds her breath, hoping he keeps his word. There are only two explanations for why Lanie is nowhere to be found, and neither of them are good:

She left with someone.

Or something terrible happened to her.

Josh admits to everyone, once again, that he was hoping for a little graduation party hook-up action, but Lanie made it clear she wasn't interested. There was something on her mind. Something serious, he says. He claims that Lanie brushed off his advances and walked into the cabin to use the bathroom. That was around midnight, Josh thinks. About ten minutes later, he saw her walking toward the woods. He figured the bathroom line was too long, so she went to the woods to pee. Lanie's phone goes straight to voicemail now.

"We need to call the police," Brainy says.

"No!" Ella cries out. "Are you crazy? Look at this place. We need to clean up first."

Beer cans and bottles and cigarette butts and wrappers litter the grounds, as if a tornado whipped up a landfill and flung its contents all over their property.

Josh barks at Ella. "How can you think about yourself at a time like this?"

"What? I'm thinking about all of us. If the cops—"

"Wait. I remember something," Reagan interrupts.

Oh God.

Here it comes.

Reagan simply can't reveal to the others what Ella thinks she's going to reveal. That would be a disaster.

Ella attempts to cut her off. "Reagan, I hardly think you were in a position to remember—"

"A biker guy was hitting on Lanie," Reagan says. "He tried to hit on me, too. Maybe he got us mixed up. Maybe he's...done something to her. That's why I kissed you, Josh. To get him to back off of me, even though you didn't believe me."

Ella breathes a small sigh of relief.

A biker guy.

She can work with that.

"Do you believe me now?" Reagan asks.

"Oh my God, Reagan. Stop making this about you. I'm going to look for her," Josh says.

"I'll go with you," Ted says.

"Maybe she sprained an ankle or broke a leg and she's stuck somewhere," Brainy suggests.

They decide they'll all look for Lanie. Starting at the edge of the woods, they fan out in different directions, searching the dense forest for their friend. After twenty minutes or so, Josh's scream stops Ella in her tracks.

"Lanie!" Josh cries out. "She's...oh my God. I think she's..."

Soon, all five of them are huddled at the edge of the ravine.

Ella looks down and sees Lanie's broken body.

A feeling of utter terror grips her and shakes her to her core, but she stuffs it down.

Ted and Brainy race down the switchback trail. Lanie's neck is twisted like a corkscrew, a gruesome injury that nobody could survive. Her lifeless body faces away from them, thankfully, so Ella doesn't have to look her in the eye.

But she imagines a blank stare.

Lanie's chocolate brown eyes.

Boring into her skull.

What have I done?

Ella's about to lose it, but she has to maintain control of her emotions; there's so much at stake. Flipping into survival mode, damage control begins.

Josh says nothing about what he knows.

Instead, he shoots her a cold death stare.

This isn't over, it says.

And that makes Ella tremble even more.

TWENTY-TWO
REAGAN

This is surreal.

Is it really happening?

Or am I dreaming?

My emotions are non-existent, and I fear that something is terribly wrong with me. Brainy and Josh climb back up from the ravine, after confirming what we all knew from looking down on her.

Lanie is dead.

None of us have cell coverage here, so we start back toward the cabin, the sober mood a stark contrast with the previous evening.

As we get closer, Josh pulls out his phone.

"What are you doing?" Ella says.

"Calling for help," Josh says. "I've got service."

"Are you crazy? We can't have the police here until we get rid of all the evidence. Who has drugs? Give them to me. *Now!*" Ella commands.

It's hard to believe that Ella's thinking about herself at a time like this. We're not even back at the cabin yet, and we just left our friend, dead in a ravine.

When I object, Ella points out that Lanie's gone, and nothing we can do now will change that. We need to save ourselves. Lanie would have wanted it that way, she says, which I tend to doubt. Nobody wants their friends to leave their dead body in a ravine while they proceed to cover their own asses.

But we all comply.

It's a fair point.

I don't want to go to jail, and neither do the rest of us.

So, I hand over my few tabs of molly as we hurry toward the cabin. Josh gives up his weed. As soon as we're back inside, Ella flushes the contraband down the toilet. Then she instructs everyone to help clean up the mess inside the cabin and around the grounds. She's already gathered the hard liquor bottles, she says, and she will wash them out and hide them in her father's tool shed.

We all get to work.

After twenty minutes or so, she gathers us again.

"Okay. Let's get our story straight."

Ella grills Josh like a prosecutor on cross-examination.

"Where was Lanie going when she left? What exactly are you going to tell the cops?" Ella asks.

"I already told you. She went to the cabin to use the bathroom. And when I saw her walk to the woods about ten minutes later, I figured she went there to pee cause the line was too long," Josh says. "That was around midnight."

"What if that biker guy did something to her?" I ask.

Ella's eyes widen and her hands fly to her hips. "No bikers were here, Reagan!"

I start to protest. "But what if—"

"Listen up," Ella says. "This party got out of hand, and that's on me. But my family could get in real trouble. All of us could, but especially me. You're my best friends. Please protect me. Nobody did anything to Lanie. That's ridiculous. It was dark. She was drinking. She must've fallen. So, here's what we'll tell the police, and we need to be on the same page. Nobody needs to say anything about her being upset or anything else. Just stick to the facts."

Ella crafts a story. Mostly, it's a true story—with a few lies of omission, a tad of embellishment, and a little tweaking on Josh's part.

It goes like this:

We had a graduation celebration. Some locals crashed the party for a bit. Ella shut it down, and the locals left. We all went to sleep. Those of us in the cabin figured Lanie was in Josh's tent. But Josh said Lanie had wandered into the woods around midnight, while the party was still going, maybe to pee because the bathroom line was long. He didn't see her after that, and he figured she was in the cabin with everybody else. In the morning, we couldn't find her. We searched the woods. We found her in the ravine. We called for help.

"And that's all we know. Are we clear?" Ella turns and looks each of us in the eye, one by one.

"Wait. What are the cops going to think?" Josh says. "It makes it look like I was the last one to see her."

"You probably were the last one to see her, Josh," Ella points out.

"We don't know that," he says.

But everyone confirms what Ella said.

None of us saw her later in the evening.

Josh reluctantly agrees to go along with it.

"Do not say anything about me trying to hook up with her. It could look like..."

We all get what it could look like, and we agree to keep that little detail out of it, as well as the biker story.

"So we're good?" Ella asks.

We all nod.

Then she calls 911.

AFTER THE POLICE LEAVE, there's a shifting of mood as we prepare to leave the camp and get on with our lives. It took hours, but after grilling all of us, they seem to be willing to let it go. Ella's parents arrived about an hour after the cops, and her father seems to have some pull with the local authorities, so it started to go better after their arrival. Ella's parents went to the morgue to help with the arrangements, whatever that means, and we're all waiting for Ella to say our goodbyes and head out.

The reality seems to be hitting everyone else, but I'm still not feeling much of anything.

Josh is the most distraught. I see him through the window. He paces the periphery of the yard, as if he's expecting Lanie to come back to life and run into his arms. Then he gets in his car and drives off without a word to any of us.

Brainy sits on the sofa in silent reflection, the only person in the living room with me.

"I've never touched a dead person before today," he says.

"I'm sure it was even worse because you knew her," I offer.

He nods.

We're both packed up and ready to go. Ted and Ella are in their bedroom, which is strange because they weren't supposed to leave until the next morning, and I wonder what they're doing. As soon as they come out, I plan to leave.

But how do we wrap up a weekend like this?

My memory is so spotty, I feel like the whole thing was a dream. That molly really messes with your head, and I'll never take it again. I could say I'll swear off alcohol, but that would probably be a lie. I'll take a break from it, though.

A long break.

All I want is to get back to Matt. To my future, and leave the past behind. But one memory is etched in my mind: I tried to kiss Josh last night. He pushed me away. People saw it. There's an explanation, but I'm not sure if anyone believes me. Hopefully, Matt will. What a waste of my time Josh was. I never meant anything to him, and I can only hope that kiss doesn't get back to Matt and ruin what I have with him. I'm so angry at Josh for not having my back, and it's killing me that I probably fed his oversized ego.

I was upset with Matt for not coming here with me this weekend, thinking he was no fun. Such a stupid fight we had. And now look what happened. If someone tells Matt about that kiss before I do, it'll ruin us. He was already jealous of Josh, from when we first got together. He might not forgive me, but I'm going to tell him. Come clean as soon as I see him. Matt was right to be concerned, and I wish I'd listened to him. Never in my wildest dreams did I think someone would die, though.

But what about Lanie? Was it really an accident? I mean, Josh said she rejected him. He was the last person to see her. And then there was that biker guy. Could he have followed her? I should have told the cops and taken the fallout from Ella. But then, I was drunk and on drugs. They could very well blame it all on me. Half the night, I was in a blackout.

No. I can't go there. It was an accident. And the police aren't stupid. If something looks off, they'll investigate. It's their job, not mine. They didn't seem too eager to poke holes in our story, so perhaps they can tell just by the way she fell that it was an accident, a fall and not a shove.

Ella and Ted come out of their bedroom, and we all say our goodbyes.

We used to make a promise.

Same time next year.

But this time, we don't.

We all know we're leaving this place behind.

Sorry, Lanie.

And goodbye.

TWENTY-THREE
ELLA

Ella's hands are shaking as she says her goodbyes and sees her friends out the door for what will surely be the last time. She knows that the camp is off-limits now for her. For all of them. How can she ever get that horrible image out of her mind of Lanie in that ravine? Those once-perfect family memories at the Parker camp, forever tainted.

And it's all Lanie's fault.

Lanie was her own worst enemy, it's true. And she's far from innocent in all of this. But they were close once. Really close. Like sisters. Like the sister she never had. Ella remembers the first time they met, when she walked into their dorm room freshman year and saw her new roommate passed out in the bottom bunk bed. Even then, Lanie had a habit of taking what she wanted without stopping to think about it.

That should be something roommates discuss, shouldn't it? Nobody wants the top bunk bed. They could have flipped for it. Or played rock paper scissors. But Lanie just saw what she wanted and took it for herself. That should have been Ella's first clue that she wasn't as innocent as she seemed.

"Hi," Lanie said, when she finally woke up, around noon. "I'm Lanie."

She went on to explain that she'd gone to a Green Day concert the night before, with some high school friends who had driven upstate for the show, and she'd gotten pretty wasted. Lanie was from Long Island and she had a cool New York City accent.

She was still dressed in her concert garb, a black CBGB's t-shirt and jeans, and Ella remembers thinking she must have been pretty gone if she couldn't even manage to take off her pants. Her make-up was sparse, but her eyeliner, smeared from sleeping in it, gave her dark brown eyes a smoky, sultry look. Or maybe it wasn't smeared from sleep and that was the look she was going for.

Lanie became a curiosity to Ella, and she forgave her for the bunk bed faux pas. Perhaps she didn't know any better. She was a scholarship student. Raised in foster care. People loved to hear Lanie's life story, especially Ella's parents, and she loved to tell it.

But truthfully, as Ella got to know her, she realized Lanie's story wasn't nearly as harrowing as she made it out to be. She did bounce around a little in the beginning, and that part of the story was always a little murky. But she landed with a solid family by the time she was five and lived with them until she aged out.

Lanie's foster mother was kind and normal, from what Ella could tell. She visited once. And although her foster dad and mom split up when Lanie was in high school, that's hardly the kind of thing that scars a child for life. But Lanie seemed bitter about the fact that the family never adopted her, and as Ella got to know Lanie better, she sensed that there was a reason the family chose to cut their ties with her.

With her heart-shaped face and haunting dark eyes, Lanie projected a veneer of vulnerability and innocence, but that masked a more formidable core. She could be manipulative, Ella realized over time. Out for herself. But she never thought Lanie would stoop as far down as she went.

Ella's not about to let Lanie derail her entire life, though. So, she holds her head high and stuffs down the crushing mix of fear, dread, anger, and remorse that's battering her soul. Ella waves as Brady and Reagan enter their cars, start them up, and drive off. Josh took off, and she'll need to deal with him later. She wasn't the only one who saw Josh kiss Lanie, so that makes him at least somewhat manageable. If they start poking around into Lanie's death, it won't be good for him, either.

Then she turns to Ted.

"So, what do we do now?" she asks.

"Nothing," he says. "We do nothing. It will all blow over. Don't worry, Ella. I've got you." Ted puts his arm around Ella's shoulder and hugs her close.

Ella and Ted are forever bonded together now.

For life.

NOW

TWENTY-FOUR
REAGAN

The months after Lanie died, I landed in a very dark place. First there was Lanie's death. Then there was my fallout with Matt, not to mention my feelings of humiliation and shame. Matt and I ended up taking a break for most of the summer, but at the time, I thought we were done for good. I'd full well planned on fessing up about Josh and my stupid kiss the moment I saw him, but Matt was so upset about the partying, I didn't want to add fuel to the fire. He didn't return my calls for two days, even after reports of Lanie's death hit the news.

He'd seen the social media posts of our weekend revelry, he said, and I'd seen them too. I have to admit, they were pretty bad. Looking at myself with my make-up smeared and that shitfaced drunken grin on my face, I felt embarrassed. Ashamed. It's one thing to act like that when you're a college freshman, but I was a graduating senior, trying to find a job. The posts didn't help. Then the story hit the news and became a cautionary tale about college students and graduation parties.

After laying into me about it, Matt ghosted me for the better part of a week. After that, it was my turn to be pissed off. I blocked him on my phone and social media. I couldn't believe that he would get that upset about one graduation weekend blowout. And I found it crushingly sad that he wasn't being more sympathetic about the death of my friend.

It was a few days after I came home that the nightmares started. I was living with my mother in Albany, temporarily, and Matt was living at his parents' house in Oswego, a few hours away. I woke in a cold sweat, and my stomach seized with dread. The sensation of being spun around lingered in my mind, as if I was Lanie. As if I was experiencing it for her. Like she was reaching back into my psyche, trying to tell me something.

Trying to tell me that her death wasn't an accident.

In my mind, the biker guy was the key to all of it. He'd hit on me. He'd hit on Lanie. We looked alike. The guilt plagued me; the fact that I'd listened to Ella and kept my mouth shut about it to the police.

I told my mother about the dream, and I was starting to tell her about my suspicions that perhaps it wasn't an accident. I didn't tell her about my lie of omission, though, which Ella strong-armed me into. Then my mom took my hand and patted it, and I stopped. I knew right then and there, before the words even left her lips, that I was better off keeping my fears to myself.

Plus, I realized that it would land back on me that I'd withheld that piece of evidence from the police if I opened up that can of worms. And if I told anyone about my lie, they'd be liable, too. I was trapped, it seemed. I couldn't come clean about it without putting myself in legal jeopardy, but I couldn't purge myself of the guilt for keeping my mouth shut to protect Ella without putting someone else in harm's way.

"Reagan. Honey. You're not the most reliable narrator, given the state of mind you were in."

Wow.

That hurt.

She continued in the same vein, basically pointing out that she was only looking out for me. And that the best thing I could do for myself and my future, she said, was to move on from this. Distance myself from the incident. Be strong. Get a job. Any job, she said. Which made me feel even worse about myself. I had a college degree. Why should I take just any job?

I got her point, though, and her concerns about me were justified. I'd plunged into a pretty deep depression. I hardly got out of bed that week. I had some benzos from a while back that were expired, but they still seemed to work. They dulled the pain temporarily, but then it would come back with a vengeance, along with the anxiety. I drank, too. Not a lot, just enough to take the edge off. But I hid it pretty well.

Finally, after a few weeks of wallowing, I cleaned myself up enough to go on some job interviews. I had a marketing degree, but all I could find was a retail job, an assistant manager position at a local home furnishing store where the owner said I could help him with product displays, which made it at least partially palatable to me. Perhaps it could be a stepping stone to something better. You have to start somewhere, and the bottom was it for me.

I couldn't get interviews anywhere else, and I assumed it was because of my social media posts. I'd deleted what I could from my accounts. But once those photos were out there, I really had no control over where they ended up. Plus, I was now associated with a raging party that led to a death, which made the news. Not the national news, but it filtered down to the Albany area.

The owner of the furniture store was an older guy named Jerry. Not as old as my parents, but too old for me. He was handsy. The kind of guy who leaned in too close when he talked to you. At first, I thought it was my imagination. But after a while, it was clear that he was hitting on me. I was still in love with Matt and missing him, but even if I wasn't, I had no interest in this Jerry guy. He had bad breath and wore jeans that bunched at the waist and had greasy hair in need of a cut.

One day, when I was getting something out of the supply closet, his hand brushed over my butt. I jumped, spun around, and lunged at him.

"Get your hands off me," I said.

His eyes widened, and he didn't apologize. "It was an accident. What the hell is wrong with you?"

We locked eyes.

I knew he was a liar.

He knew that I knew, but we didn't speak of it anymore.

At the end of the day, he called me into his office and told me he was letting me go. I'd been late a few times, including that morning. He used that as the reason for my termination, but I knew the truth. He was worried I'd file some kind of complaint, and this was a preemptive strike. I didn't argue. It was a stupid job, anyway. I wasn't even planning to put it on my resume.

But when I got home, my mother was furious. She didn't believe me about the come-on and basically called me a liar. Not in so many words, but she implied that I'd imagined it and that I was making excuses for being late to work. She told me I needed to get help—which, of course, was true.

Looking back, I'm pretty sure that I didn't want to die that night. What I wanted was to be free of the pain. To be at peace. To sleep through the night without having that recurring nightmare wake me and shake me to my core.

So rather than a half a benzo, I took the rest of them.

And I slept pretty well.

So well, I woke up in the hospital.

The first face I saw was Matt's.

That was the start of my journey back from the darkness.

It was a long road, but I made it.

Until I had Danny.

Then the feelings of dread came back.

And now I know why.

TWENTY-FIVE
REAGAN

I've been lying here for over an hour as memories come flooding back in, along with the raging storm outside my bedroom window.

Here's what I know.

Lanie was pregnant.

She was upset that night.

Josh was the last person to see her.

But Lanie didn't want to hook up with Josh, so, obviously, he wasn't the father of her child. Of course, it could have been anyone. Some guy none of us knew about. A secret romance, though. She wasn't seeing anyone that we knew about.

And the only person I can think of is Ted.

What if Lanie and Ted were having an affair?

How would Ella take that?

Not well.

I think of Ella's demeanor down in the ravine. She was genuinely broken up. Guilt will do that to a person.

Sorry, Lanie, she said.

Sorry for what?

The thing is, Ella's not stupid. If she murdered Lanie ten years ago, why would she gather us here? What would be the point? If she did murder her, she's gotten away with it. Why bring it all up again?

And what about Ted?

Could Ted have pushed Lanie over the cliff?

He stood to lose a lot if Ella broke it off with him. A college dropout with no future to speak of. Ted's done very well for himself, riding on the coattails of Ella's father. Ted seems quite close to him. And Ted would know that losing Ella would mean losing his ticket to a better life.

But would he kill for it?

Of course, there's always the possibility that the biker guy did something to Lanie. Maybe he waited and watched from the woods, hoping to snare his prey. Me. Her. Perhaps it didn't matter. But if he was some kind of serial killer, there would have been more missing women over the years, wouldn't there?

And what about Josh? He's got a big ego. She rejected him. And now I know that Lanie broke up with Josh, not the other way around. I remember that he was adamant about the fact that we could not tell the cops that he hit on her that night and that Lanie rejected him. He was worried about how that would look.

Because it doesn't look good, does it?

There's always the possibility that Lanie did this to herself, of course. That she was so despondent and alone and depressed, she ended her own life.

I close my eyes and let it all swirl in my mind.
A flash of memory returns.
I was lying in this bed.
Voices drifted in from outside my window.
Lanie.
Lanie's voice.
"I'm having this baby," it says.
Her tone is forceful and determined.
Not the tone of a woman about to hurl herself off a cliff.
It's loud and clear in my mind.
It wasn't a suicide.
But that's all I've got.

BRADY IS SITTING on the sofa when I come out of my room. It's early afternoon, and rain is soaking the mountain, likely making the drive down treacherous. The sound of a thousand high-pressure fire hoses blasts the front of the cabin. It's coming from the south, and the cabin faces that direction. Outside, the visibility is almost zero, and I wonder if Ted will even be able to get back here tonight.

Wind whips through the crevices, and I pull my cardigan tight around me. The whistling could drive you crazy, especially with no music or TV to drown it out. I imagine mudslides and boulders and streams spilling out over their banks, and my stomach tenses. The water comes in waves, and while the wind isn't too bad, the occasional strong gust rips in, and we hear a crash in the distance. I wonder if my car will get damaged and I won't be able to go home, even if it stops. The storm is closing in on us, that's for sure. I've never been particularly claustrophobic, but I'm starting to get a little panicky.

And if Josh hurt himself.

If he's stranded somewhere...

I don't even want to think about it.

I can't stand him, but still.

Water. I need a glass of water.

"Is Ted back yet?" I ask, making my way over to the kitchen to quench my thirst.

The thought of being stuck here. Trapped in this cabin. It heightens all my senses, and my basic needs seem more urgent. More pressing, like if there was only one bottle of water left in this room, I'd rip it right out of Brady's hand and chug it down. I can see how people turn on each other in these kinds of situations, and my heart races as I think about how ugly it could get, especially with all of us so tense to begin with.

"No," Brady says.

"No sign of Josh, I take it?"

"Nope."

Brady informs me that Ella went to lie down in her room. It's clear we are going to be stuck here for another night together. At least we haven't lost power yet. I know it's a risk telling Brady what I remembered, but I need to bounce it off of someone. My imagination is running wild. It's possible we're in danger, and I need to give Brady a heads-up.

Sitting across from him with my water, I take a chance. "Brady. I have to tell you something. Something I remembered from that night. But it's important to me that you keep it to yourself for now. Can you do that?"

"I'm not sure about this. You know I don't like to gossip."

"It's not gossip, Brady. It could be important. And I don't want to be the only one who knows this. But you can't tell Ella and Ted what I remembered. I'm afraid it could be dangerous for me. It's about Lanie."

Brady rolls his eyes but agrees to my terms, and I tell him what I heard Lanie say about being pregnant. Fearing he might push back and try to tell me I was out of my mind and on drugs that night, I brace myself for a skeptical look of scorn to flash across Brady's face.

But that's not what happens.

His brow furrows.

"Hmm," he says.

Hmm?

But I give him space and don't press him.

After a minute or so, he elaborates. "That actually makes sense. Because I wasn't drinking much, and Lanie seemed pretty sober to me. I even saw her spilling out a cup of beer when nobody was looking. I thought it was odd, but..."

"But it makes sense if she was pregnant and she didn't want anyone to know about it."

"Right," Brady says.

"You see what that means?" I offer.

He narrows his eyes on me. "What are you getting at, Reagan?"

"She probably didn't stumble off a cliff that night. She obviously wasn't drunk."

His eyes widen, and his face seems to go a shade paler. "Oh shit," Brady says. "You're right."

"Why didn't you speak up that day? If you thought Lanie was sober?" I ask.

Brady sighs. "I mean, she was the type who could hold her liquor. Not like you. It didn't really occur to me that maybe she wasn't drunk. Not until now. And I guess if I'm being honest, I didn't want to rock the boat."

"It seems we're all complicit in one way or another," I say.

He nods. "The five of us. Bonded by guilt. If I had it to do over..."

"Well," I say. "Maybe we'll get a second chance to do it over. If Lanie wasn't drinking, that means that—"

My head turns to see Ella entering the room. She forces her face into a polite smile, but only after I catch a glimpse of what I could only interpret as a look of sheer panic wash over her.

Ella changes the subject. "So sorry I dozed off. I'm getting worried about Ted. He should have been back by now."

I'm not sure which possibility is more terrifying to me. The fact that she may have heard what Brady and I were talking about. Or the fact that she's pretending that she didn't.

We hear a car drive up, but it doesn't sound like Ted's car. Rushing to the front window, we glance out through the sheets of water pounding the front lawn, turning it into a chocolate factory. The three of us spot a modified rescue vehicle that looks like a cross between an ATV and a military jeep, raised high with giant tires and a rack on the back with equipment.

It stops in front of the cabin and three men jump out.

They are wrapped in rain ponchos.

Dashing for the door, they enter.
One of them is Ted.
The other two are police officers.
"We found Josh," Ted says. "He's dead."

TWENTY-SIX
ELLA

Ella sinks into the floor, wishing she could disappear. Wishing she had more time to assess the situation and figure out what to do from here. It's completely plausible that Josh stumbled and fell in this weather, but she knows how it will look to the authorities. One tragic death at a college blowout ten years ago can be explained.

But now this?

Her father's connections might not save them this time.

"Where did you find him?" Ella asks.

Ted speaks first. "He was—"

"No." One of the officers holds up a hand and stops Ted; an older-looking burly man with dark, beady eyes. He takes off his rain poncho hood to reveal a bald head with thick forehead creases that resemble earthworms. In a word, he's menacing. He seems to be in charge.

"This is a suspicious death investigation. I'm Officer Branson. You'll come with me," he says to Ted. "We have more questions for you. We need to search the victim's room and look through his belongings. Which room was he staying in? Officer Thompson will search his room."

The victim.

Ella shows Officer Thompson, a younger guy with sandy brown hair and a smaller build, to the room where Josh was staying.

Branson turns to us and motions to the sofa before he enters the master bedroom with Ted. "The rest of you, stay there. Don't go anywhere," he barks.

The three of them seat themselves. Ella and Reagan on the sofa. Brady in an armchair across from them.

Josh is dead.

The police are here.

Well, Ella had ten good years.

Ten years of being a happy family. Giving birth to two wonderful little boys. Her mother and father, the doting grandparents. She and Ted, making their mark in the world. A perfect life on the outside, but on some level, Ella knew she was living on borrowed time. The secrets, nibbling on her insides like a fast-growing cancer. Taking a little more of her every day. If it all comes out, perhaps she'll finally be at peace.

Perhaps that's why she organized this gathering to begin with. On some subconscious level, she wanted it all to come out.

Reagan looks pale, like she might pass out.

Brady is hard to read.

"I don't understand," Reagan says. "What happened?"

Ella shakes her head. "I know as much as you do," she says.

Which isn't quite true. Ella fears she knows what

happened and it seizes her with a feeling bordering on sheer panic, but she's not certain, and she's fighting to keep it inside. She's holding on to the slim hope that maybe, just maybe, Josh slipped and fell and the police are acting like this because they are suspicious of two deaths happening at their cabin.

But would they even know about Lanie's death ten years ago? It's not likely to be the same officers. They probably haven't been in touch with their headquarters. They are in the middle of a hurricane, or maybe it's been downgraded to a tropical storm.

So why would they be calling this death suspicious? She doesn't recall that happening a decade ago. Ella feels like she's missing something, and she's desperate to talk to Ted.

Why would they be detaining him unless...

No, she can't go there.

Brady speaks up. "This isn't a coincidence, Ella. And I think you know more than you're letting on. I can see it in your face. Do you know something about what happened to Lanie ten years ago? Or what happened to Josh today? Why did you even bring us here this weekend?"

Ella's jaw stiffens. "I'd be careful about going down that road if I were you, Brady. In fact, out of all of us, you're the one who seemed to have the biggest beef with Josh this weekend. I saw the way you looked at him. We all did. And you were out on a run when he was. Means. Motive. Opportunity. You've got it all. So, you really want to go there? You really want to start turning on each other?"

"Don't threaten him," Reagan says. "Brady's right. Something's up. I saw you and Josh huddled in the kitchen, and you seemed upset with him. Why? Were the two of you up to something? Something that would enrage your husband? Because Ted was out of the cabin when Josh was out running, too. Brady's not the only one with means, motive, and opportunity. And Ted's the one being questioned, not Brady."

"Well, Reagan had a blowout with Josh, too," Brady points out. "I wasn't the only one."

"Thanks, Brady," Reagan says. "Way to have my back. I guess it's every man for himself around here."

Ella lets out a long sigh. "Let's walk this back a little," she says. "We don't even know if it was a homicide. The officer called it a suspicious death. And one thing we know for sure is that the three of us had nothing to do with whatever happened to Josh, because we were all in the cabin together."

Reagan and Brady look to each other, and Ella senses a joint attack coming.

"What did those texts say again?" Brady asks.

Ella pulls out her phone and reads them, reiterating what she told them before, about Josh saying he needed some time for himself.

"Let me see them," Reagan says.

Ella's teeth clench.

Ungrateful bitch.

She shows the texts to Brady and Reagan.

"Satisfied now?" Ella says.

Then she crosses her arms, leans back, and turns away from them. It's too late. They've already turned on each other.

Survival of the fittest.

And Ella's a survivor.

TWENTY-SEVEN
REAGAN

Josh is dead.
　Lanie is dead.
　Ten years ago, Lanie was pregnant.
　Something was going on with Ella and Josh, this weekend and ten years ago.
　But what does it all mean?
　How is this all connected?
　At least I no longer have doubts about myself. I was mad at Lanie that night, but I didn't push her off a cliff or anything. Someone did, though. Now, I'm sure of it.
　Ella says that the three of us couldn't have done anything to Josh because we were all here in the cabin. But that's not quite true, because Ella was in her room for a pretty long time. She could have climbed out the window without us knowing, especially with the downpour we were having, muffling the sound.
　Again, though. I go back to motive. What was the motive?

Love and money.

Those are the big ones.

So let's start with love. Lanie was pregnant with someone's baby. If it was Ted's baby, that explains a lot. Maybe it was simple. Ella was jealous. She killed Lanie out of jealousy. On the other hand, an affair between Ella and Josh is also possible, based on what I've seen. Could Ted have slept with Lanie in retaliation? Could it all be some twisted Shakespearean tragedy? Ella kills Lanie for sleeping with her husband, and Ted kills Josh for sleeping with his wife? That all seems a little too far-fetched.

I move on to money.

Lanie is murdered, for what? Was there money involved? What if it was Ted's baby? Ted would want to silence Lanie so Ella wouldn't find out. Ella is Ted's golden goose. He couldn't afford to lose her. Lanie was penniless, and Ted was a college dropout. So, he killed Lanie to shut her up.

But why kill Josh?

Did he suspect something?

Were they paying Josh for his silence?

I'm dying to talk to Brady alone, to see what he makes of all of it. And I go over in my mind what I know for sure, as we sit in uncomfortable silence.

Because I can't trust anyone here today. I can only rely on what I remember, not what anyone told me, including Josh or Brady.

So, what do I know, for sure?

Lanie was pregnant. I heard her say that outside my bedroom window.

She wanted to keep the baby.

Ella and Josh had some tension between them, ten years ago and now.

I heard a scream in the woods.

A biker guy was hitting on Lanie that night.

I have a memory of some guy grabbing Lanie and spinning her around, but I can't see a face, and it feels as if that might have been a dream.

All a bunch of random memories, and they don't seem to be in any logical order in my mind. But one thing comes back to me now. I remember walking over to Lanie and Josh that night. I was trying to warn Lanie about the snake man and explain to Josh why I tried to kiss him. I remember being pissed off because they wouldn't believe me, but then I probably wasn't making a whole lot of sense. Josh said they were in the middle of something. So, it's possible that Josh knew more than he was supposed to know about Lanie and her baby, and that's why he was eager to get rid of me.

The best-case scenario:

Lanie was upset. Maybe about the baby, or Josh, or whatever. She went into the woods and fell to her death. This weekend, Josh felt guilty about...something. Maybe Lanie told him who the father was and he wasn't supportive? He felt bad for hitting on her when she needed him to be a friend? It got to him this weekend. He foolishly went out for a hike in the rain. He slipped and fell to his death. And as I'm going over it in my mind, I realize that's pretty implausible.

The worst-case scenario:

Lanie was pregnant, and the father was someone it shouldn't have been. Ten years ago, she was murdered for that. Josh figured it out. And then he was murdered, too.

Unfortunately, the worst-case scenario seems much more possible. And I can only thank my lucky stars that the police are here, because I'm starting to remember things too—and I could be next.

But one part of this scenario doesn't add up at all. If Ted murdered Josh and tried to make it look like an accident, why did he go looking for him? Why not simply leave him there to be found, a casualty of the storm?

Officer Thompson enters the living room.

We all turn to him.

And what comes out of his mouth shatters all of my preconceptions into a million pieces.

"I found a suicide note," the officer reports. "We need to talk about your friend's state of mind before he went for that jog." Then he knocks on the door of the master bedroom.

Ella's jaw drops. From the look on her face, this is a shock to her, too.

I had it all wrong, and I'm shaken to my core.

Josh killed himself?

But why?

TWENTY-EIGHT
REAGAN

Officer Thompson dropped the bomb on us and went into the bedroom where Ted is still being questioned by the menacing one whose name I forget, leaving the three of us sitting in stunned silence.

It's Brady who speaks first. "I don't believe it," he says, shaking his head. "Josh would never kill himself."

I don't buy it either, but I'm not about to say that out loud. "Well," I offer, "you never can tell what's going on inside a person's head. And with men, they tend to not give much of a warning."

"I guess you would know," Ella says.

I sit up and shoot back at her. "What's that supposed to mean?"

"Nothing," she says. "It's just...your history."

"Look, Ella. I didn't try to kill myself, and I don't know why you told that to Brady. Did Matt tell you that?"

She shrugs. "Not in so many words."

"Let me set the record straight. I took a gummy that was

too strong, on top of my other meds. It was a mistake, not a suicide attempt."

Ella nods along. "I see. Well, it makes sense. You've always had trouble coping, and you have a self-destructive streak."

"Oh, no, Ella. That's where you're wrong. I'm not self-destructive. I'm a survivor. Just like you."

We hold each other's gaze for a long moment.

Ted and the two officers come out of the bedroom and break the spell.

They send Ted out into the living room and call Brady in.

Brady rises and looks over at Ella, but she can't seem to look him in the eye. Rather, she stares off into the distance, her mouth slightly open, as if she's about to speak, but she doesn't.

I want to disappear. To vanish. To be invisible. I've got nothing to say to either of them, so I move to the far end of the sofa and curl into myself, hoping they will leave me alone. I would move to the seat across from them, but then I'd have to look them in the face, and that would be worse.

"We need to talk," Ted says to Ella.

Thankfully, Ted takes his wife by the hand and leads her into the kitchen.

They speak in hushed tones, and I can only make out a few words. Ella is facing me, so I can read her expressions, and somewhat see the words on her lips, but with Ted, I don't have the visual cues.

Ted says something about the timeline, and Branson, the officer, questioning him about it.

Then something about Brady.

Ella's eyes widen and her hand flies to her mouth.

Ted places a hand on her shoulder.

Ted is shaking his head. He's freaked out, that much is evident.

"I think I need a lawyer," Ted says, which I hear loud and clear.

Ella mumbles something under her breath.

Ted lets out a long sigh.

The rain had let up, but it starts again, pounding down on the cabin in thundering waves.

A strong gust of wind slams something against the side of the cabin and it crashes into the kitchen wall with a loud bang. The sound of glass shattering fills our ears. All three of us turn to the sound. A tree branch pokes through the window, and my pulse starts to pound. There are so many trees around. What if a really big one crashes down? Could it cave in the roof?

Then the lights go out, darkening an already dim day.

It's still light enough outside that we can sort of see okay, but this means that the food will start to spoil, and we might have to be here overnight with no electricity. Part of me wants to confess to something—anything—so the cops will take me with them and not leave me here with the three of them. I don't trust any of them. Not even Brady. Not after that veiled threat he made to me and the way he threw me under the bus before.

After a few minutes, the officers return to the living room with Brady.

"We have a backlog of calls, and we need to get on the search and rescue," Officer Branson says. "Especially now that people have lost power. We've got vulnerable populations around town. You'll want to board that up." He motions to the kitchen window.

And then he proceeds to inform Brady and Ted that the two of them need to go with them down to the station for further questioning. "We'll take statements from you two ladies later."

"But you said it was a suicide," Ella protests.

"No," Officer Branson says. "Officer Thompson said he found a suicide note, which was not something he needed to disclose."

Officer Branson shoots daggers at Officer Thompson, apparently a rookie, who hangs his head.

This stops me in my tracks.

The police found a suicide note, but they don't seem to believe it was a suicide.

What did it say?

Did it have something to do with Lanie and her death?

"Are they under arrest?" Ella asks.

"Not at this time, no. But they still need to come with us," Officer Branson says.

"You can't make them go with you if they're not under arrest," Ella points out. But her tone isn't forceful. She says it more like a question.

Officer Branson tilts his head down and peers at her, then he looks over at the rookie with the big mouth and shrugs. "That could be arranged."

Brady's eyes widen. "Ella! It's fine. I want to go," Brady says. "I have nothing to hide. I want to help."

Ted chimes in. "Yeah, honey, it's fine. We want to cooperate."

And it starts to sink in where that leaves me.

My stomach churns and my throat feels as if it's closing up on me.

The two of us.

Stuck inside this cabin.

With no electricity and no phone service.

Ella and I catch each other's eyes and lock onto one another for a long moment, both of us knowing what this will mean.

At least it's one on one.

I've got a fighting chance.

I'm a survivor.

But so is she.

TWENTY-NINE
ELLA

Ted can handle this, Ella tells herself. They've been in tight spots with the police before. But the last time, she knew what she was up against. This time, she's positively perplexed. A suicide note? That came out of left field. And she has no idea what it says.

"So, Ella," Reagan says. "I guess it's just you and me now."

Ella replies, "Looks like it. Let me get you a flashlight. It's nearing four o'clock, and it will be dark in a few hours. We should have plenty of food and water. The storm will pass soon, so you'll be able to leave in the morning and get home safely."

"That's the hope," Reagan says.

Ella fetches the flashlight and some ice water for the two of them. Then she places a glass of water in front of Reagan and shrugs. "We need to stay hydrated."

Reagan smiles. "Seems like an odd thing to worry about

at a time like this." But she drinks down half a glass. "Wow, you're right. I was pretty thirsty."

Ella feels her out. "How are you doing about all of this? I know Josh meant something to you once."

Reagan looks at her, puzzled. "I'm feeling shocked and sad, like the rest of us, but not any more so. What are you getting at?"

"Nothing, Reagan," Ella says. "I'm getting at nothing."

It's going to be a long night.

After a few minutes, Reagan continues. "Do you know what happened? How Josh died?"

Ella nods. "Yeah, Ted told me. He shot himself. In the head."

Reagan's jaw drops. "Josh shot himself? With a gun? Josh had a gun? He didn't jump or fall or something?"

Ella lets out a breath. And the enormity of that revelation is just starting to sink in. "No. Which is why the police acted like they did. A gun always raises suspicion. Naturally, Ted's very shaken up, after finding him like that."

"Does Ted know what was in the note?" she asks.

Ella shakes her head. "No."

Reagan stands and starts to pace, and it makes Ella more nervous. "But why would Josh kill himself? I mean, do you think he felt...do you think he did something to Lanie that night?" she asks.

Ella sighs. "I would like to think not. At least not intentionally. But then you never know. Maybe it was an accident. Maybe after Lanie rejected him, he went after her and she fell."

Reagan nods. "They could have argued," she says. "I saw them that night. In some kind of intense discussion."

Reagan tells Ella again about kissing Josh, which Ella already knew about. Reagan claims she only did it to get away from the biker guy who was hitting on her, but that Josh didn't believe her. Reagan says she went to warn Lanie about the biker guy, who was hitting on Lanie later in the evening, perhaps confusing the two of them, which could happen, especially in the dark.

"I didn't see a biker guy with Lanie," Ella says. "But yeah, I guess anything is possible."

"When I went to warn her, Josh said they were in the middle of something," Reagan reveals. "And he was annoyed by my interruption. Acted like a real asshole, if I'm being honest."

Ella shrugs. "Unfortunately, it all adds up," Ella says. "Josh obviously wanted her back. He admitted that he tried to hook up with her that night. She rejected him. I guess he didn't take it well. And the ceremony this weekend, it must have been too much for him."

Reagan shakes her head. "So, all these years, we thought it was an accident. And for ten years, Josh was holding it in. I could see how this weekend could have pushed him to the brink. All that guilt. I bet it wasn't intentional, though. Josh is a lot of things, but he's not a murderer. I can't believe he would have done it on purpose. Just pushed her off a cliff and left her there to die."

Ella knows that Josh did not kill Lanie on purpose. In fact, she knows that Josh didn't kill Lanie at all, and she knows exactly who did. But she never thought he'd go this far. The plan was to give Josh an ultimatum; to rid them of the problem.

Neutralize him, were his exact words.

Not murder him.

Part of her knew what that could mean, she realizes in hindsight, but a bigger part of her believed it would be a warning. That he wouldn't harm Josh.

But to do it with a gun?

Making it look like a suicide?

That makes no sense.

Guns can be traced, and they always raise red flags. It seems crazy risky to try and fake a suicide, so Ella considers that maybe it's true. Maybe Josh did kill himself. Perhaps he had more of a conscience than he let on, and Ella knows firsthand how guilt can eat away at a person.

But what did he say in the suicide note?

That, in and of itself, is enough to ruin her for life.

Now she's stuck in this cabin with Reagan, and she can only hope that Reagan's memories stay safely tucked away in that troubled mind of hers. This gathering was the worst idea ever. She should have let sleeping dogs lie.

"It's all so sad," Reagan says.

"It really is," Ella agrees.

Ella and Reagan leave it at that.

Josh and Lanie had some kind of altercation.

Lanie fell off the edge and died.

Josh carried the guilt for a decade.

It finally got to him, so he confessed.

And then he took his own life.

Ella senses that Reagan doesn't believe it for a minute. She's playing along, trying to get through this weekend alive. But Reagan's memories are starting to surface, and Ella needs them to stay buried. The last thing she wants is another death on her conscience.

And if Reagan remembers that Lanie was pregnant?
Well then, Reagan could very well be next.

THIRTY

REAGAN

"I've scraped together some dinner for us," Ella calls out from behind my closed bedroom door.

"Okay. Give me a few minutes," I say.

Ella replies. "Take your time. It's not like we're going anywhere."

That sounds ominous, but I try not to read too much into it.

After that startling revelation about Josh, I told her I needed to take a nap. But of course, I was too nervous to sleep. I doubt I'll sleep all night. The rain has let up, so I'm sure the roads will be okay in the morning. Part of me thinks I should risk it and go soon, maybe right after we eat, but I don't want to alarm her.

Images of Danny fill my mind, and I struggle to recall his scent and the feel of his warm little body in my arms. I can't believe it's only been a day or so since I've seen him. It feels like a lifetime that I've been away. What if something happens to me and I don't make it out of here? He'll have to grow up without a mother. I can't let that happen. I need to play it cool, until it's safe to leave.

None of this makes any sense to me, though. How could Ted have found Josh and staged a suicide in the short time he was away? And why kill him in that manner? Why not just push him off a cliff or something and pretend that he jumped? It seems so risky to stage a suicide with a gun. Can't the police tell if someone actually shot themselves? And can't the gun be traced?

Josh wasn't a very good person. He surely had enemies. Could someone else have done this to him? Or could he really have done this to himself? But while he wasn't a good person, I can't see him as a murderer. And if he'd actually killed Lanie in some accidental altercation, he'd have felt guilty about it. Of that much, I'm certain.

And what about the tension I saw between Ella and Josh? That could be the key to figuring it all out. Josh knew something, I'm sure of it. That has to factor into it. But I need to be careful not to pry and keep all my suspicions to myself.

I shouldn't have come here. I've paid my debt to Lanie, and now I realize that I'm a mother, first and foremost. And if I do get out of here alive, I'll put my family first, no matter what. This is the promise I make to the universe or God or whoever is pulling the strings up there, although I only selectively believe in a higher power when it suits me and my back is against the wall. This time, though, I promise it will be different. If I make it out alive, I'll put Danny's needs above anything else.

I can't stay in my room forever, and I'm hungry, so I grab my flashlight and open my bedroom door. "So, what's on the menu?" I ask, trying to keep it casual as I stroll over to my dining table.

"Turkey and avocado sandwiches on wheat bread and a side salad," Ella replies.

Ella's in the kitchen, but the food is set out on the table. I see she's pulled out the branch and taped up the window with cardboard. I should have offered to help her.

The cardboard is soaked though and water dribbles down to the butcher block countertop, but for the most part, it's keeping the rain out. They'll have some damage to contend with. It's chillier though, with the wind coming in through the makeshift barrier.

We don't have any firewood. Ella's dad said the store was sold out of artificial logs. It's still warm enough that we can do without heat for a night. I'm sure it will get colder tonight, though. I'm wearing three layers right now, and that's about all I have.

Ella's placed some lit candles on the dining table, which flicker in the darkness. Two flashlights sit on the kitchen counter pointing upward, casting small rings of light on the ceiling. I can make out her form, but I can't see her face.

"Looks very romantic," I say.

Ella laughs.

"You want a glass of wine?" she asks.

Of course I do.

And I should probably say no. But what the hell? If she's going to kill me, I may as well have a little buzz on.

"Just a little," I say. "For old time's sake."

"For old time's sake," she says. "That sounds good."

Ella pours us two half-glasses of pinot noir, places them on the wooden farm table, and sits across from me. I place my flashlight face up on the end of the dining table to give us some more illumination.

Never before have I seen such total darkness outside a window. No street lights. Nothing but blackness as far as the eye can see. The rain has slowed to a steady pattering, with occasional gusts of wind reminding us not to grow complacent.

"To old times," I say.

We toast. The light from my flashlight falls up and down again, cascading down Ella's face in selective spots, giving her a haunted look.

What's lurking in those memories of yours, Ella?

From the night Lanie died.

From all of it.

Maybe it's the slight alcohol buzz, but after a few minutes of awkward small talk, we start to unwind and find our groove, and it almost feels like it did years ago, back when we were young and innocent with our whole lives ahead of us.

We talk about how we all met. Brady and I were the last ones to be looped into the inner circle. Lanie and Ella were dorm mates, and I got to know Ella later, in my English class, when we studied together for a midterm. Josh and Brady were roommates but Josh and Ted were fast friends, next-door neighbors. Brady wasn't too into the whole party scene, so at first, he tried to keep his distance. But over time, the six of us meshed into a tight little group, and freshman year, we were inseparable.

"Remember that party when Brady drank too much and passed out? I thought we might have killed him," Ella says.

"I actually don't remember it."

"Right," Ella says.

I shrug.

As I said, I'm not proud of how crazy I partied back in my early college days. And from Ella's comment, I wonder if she wasn't perhaps pacing herself back then, a bit more than she let on. If that's true, she probably remembers more than I care to know.

About me.

About everyone.

See, Ella's not foolish. Not like me. She likes to be in control, and drugs and alcohol certainly don't jive with that desire.

We continue, talking about the fact that Brady never drank that much again. We called him our "designated driver," even when we weren't actually driving anywhere. It was a figure of speech. He was the cooler. The one who tapped you on the shoulder and took the shot out of your hand when you were on the verge of making an idiot of yourself. At least, he tried. With our group, it must have been hard to keep up.

But now I see that Ella was a bit of an observer, too. And I wonder how much she knows, and how much she suspects, about me. I realize now that she gathered us here this weekend for just that purpose. To observe. To watch us interact. To gauge how much we know.

Josh knew too much for his own good, I suspect.

But what about me?

How much does she suspect that I know?

"Tell me something," Ella says.

My stomach lurches.

"Um, sure, Ella. What is it?"

"Why did you make out with Ted?"

My eyes nearly pop out of my head.

She's still pissed about this?

"I, um, it was nothing, Ella."

"You knew I liked him, Reagan. I confided in you about that. Up in this cabin, in fact. At the end of freshman year. So I'll ask you again. Why did you make out with Ted?"

I swallow. My throat feels as if it's about to close up.

But I realize it's a fair question, and one I've never really asked myself.

Why *did* I make out with Ted?

I mean, I obviously did it to stick it to her.

But why?

After a few minutes, I blow out a breath and respond. "I think I was jealous of you," I say.

Her brow furrows. "Jealous of me?" Ella says.

"It was all so effortless for you. You were so poised. So popular. And I wanted to be close to you. So, when you started to ditch me for Lanie, it hurt my feelings. I'm saying this in hindsight, Ella. At the time, I thought it just sort of happened. But now, I can see that I probably did it somewhat intentionally. To get back at you. And I'm sorry. I'm really sorry."

Ella's shoulders sink and her face softens. "Thank you for an honest answer, Reagan. I accept your apology," she says. "And I'm sorry, too. I'm sorry I ditched you for Lanie. That was a big mistake."

"What do you mean by that?" I ask.

Her eyes widen. "Oh, nothing," she says. "To tell you the truth, I always felt like the odd man out. It seemed like you two had some connection. Something I couldn't penetrate.

You two grew closer over the first few years, and Lanie and I grew apart. I suppose with three women, it can get a little competitive."

"Until she went with Josh," I point out.

Ella rolls her eyes. "Yes, that was a real douchebag move, I'll give you that. I bet it made you very angry."

I shrug.

Is this where she's going?

Trying to cast some blame on me?

"Nah," I say. "Josh wasn't marriage material. Lanie did me a favor."

Ella nods in agreement. "I suppose she did. Especially in light of the fact that he might be a murderer."

"You really think he killed Lanie and then killed himself?" I ask.

"I have no idea," she says. "I know as much as you do."

I doubt that.

"But it's not nice to speak ill of the dead, as they say." I throw up my hands, then take a sip of my wine.

Ella's head tilts to one side.

There's a smirk on her face now.

"That's what they say." She pauses.

"But I won't tell if you won't."

THIRTY-ONE
ELLA

Ella reminds herself to be careful as she studies Reagan's expressions in the dim, flickering candlelight. She makes sure to take one sip of wine for Reagan's three sips, so as to keep her wits about her while her friend is loosening up. It's a delicate dance Ella's performing. Trying to get Reagan to open up to her about what she knows by throwing her some breadcrumbs, but not giving away more than she needs to.

"So, what do you want to tell me?" Reagan asks. "I'll never tell. Cross my heart."

"Oh gosh, I was joking. There's nothing you don't already know. You knew Lanie better than I did, especially toward the end."

"Not really," Reagan says. "She lived with you, not me. She spent holidays with your family. We were close in the beginning. But after she went with Josh so soon after he ditched me, it wasn't the same between us. And I hope you don't feel that way about me and that stupid kiss with Ted."

Ella shakes her head. "That was different. Ted and I had never been together at that point. He was fair game."

"Well, I think the only reason he went for me is that he didn't think he could get you. Or maybe to make you jealous. Josh was always flirting with you. I guess we all thought you two would hook up at some point. It seemed sort of inevitable to the rest of us."

Ella rolls her eyes. "Josh. Well, yeah, he was...persistent, I'll give him that."

"Now tell the truth, Ella, since we're in the vault here. Did you and Josh ever..."

Ella's trying to read Reagan. A curious look sits on her face, but it could be her way of trying to throw the blame for what happened to Josh back on them.

Does she believe that Ted did something to Josh out of jealousy?

Or are we just sharing girl talk like old friends?

"Josh and me? Oh, hell no. He's not my type at all. I need to be the one who turns heads. We both know that about me. It would never have worked with Josh. But I think he and Lanie, well, that could have been something."

Reagan shrugs. "Not according to Josh. Lanie blew him off that night. I wonder if she was seeing someone else senior year."

Ella bristles and then regains her composure, hoping that Reagan didn't notice. "Did she say something to you about that, or is that just a hunch?" Ella says.

"No, she never talked to me about guys after our falling out about Josh. This whole time, though, I thought Josh dumped Lanie. But I found out this weekend it was the other way around. Did you know that?"

"Um, yeah. She told me not to tell you. To spare your feelings," Ella tells her.

"Well, that was nice of her. Anyway, she was working part-time and going to school, after your dad offered her that internship over the summer. It seemed like she was focused on finishing college and launching her career. Like she wasn't at all interested in dating. I guess that's another reason we drifted. I was with Matt. You were with Ted. Lanie was single."

"Right. We had some fun double dates, didn't we? Ted and Matt got along pretty well, from what I recall. It's a shame we lost touch. We need to see each other more often. We're not even an hour apart. There's no excuse for how we've drifted. Except for Lanie. And the awful memory of that weekend. But we can't let that tarnish the next ten years."

"Right. To staying in touch," Reagan says.

They toast again.

Ella circles back to their conversation about Lanie. "You would think, if she wasn't seeing anyone, she'd have taken the chance for one last hook-up with Josh. I mean, where's the harm? She wasn't above it. We all know that. But then here I am, speaking ill of the dead."

"Well, let's put a positive spin on it. Lanie was a liberated woman who refused to be slut shamed," Reagan says. "Is that better?"

"That's perfect." Ella presses on, seeing if she can get Reagan to spill what she knows, if in fact she has remembered anything important. "So why would this liberated woman who wasn't seeing anyone give up a night of fun? Unless, of course, there was someone else."

Reagan smirks. "Well, seeing how we're speaking ill of the dead tonight, I could see why Lanie would give him a pass. Knowing Josh, it might not have been too fun. At least not for Lanie."

Ella's eyes pop open and she lets out a little chuckle in spite of herself. "Oh my God. I need details, Reagan. Please. Are you telling me that Josh was lousy in bed? Maybe on some level, I sensed it. What was it? Erectile disfunction? Premature ejaculation?"

Reagan seems to blush a little, but it's hard to tell in this light. "Well, more the latter, but not in the way you mean. He was pretty self-absorbed, if you get my drift. It was premature, yeah. For me." She shrugs.

Ella smiles. "Oh, that's hysterical. Good to know I didn't miss anything," Ella says. "But why do you think you fell so hard for him, then?"

Reagan sighs. "I didn't know any better, until I met Matt. I thought they were all like that. I mean, most young guys are pretty clueless, aren't they?"

Ella shrugs. "I'm not sure. Ted and I have always been compatible in that department. I know people thought we were an odd couple. But we work, especially in the sack. But what about Lanie? Do you think she had some secret lover she kept from us?"

"Like I said, we didn't talk about guys after Josh. But did she tell you something, Ella?" Reagan asks. "Is that what you're getting at? If she did, please. By all means. Dish! We've come this far tonight. Let's really drive a nail in their coffins."

"Me? No." Ella shakes her head. "I know nothing about Lanie's love life. Like I said, we weren't that close anymore."

"I guess we'll never know," Reagan offers.

"And it's not really important," Ella adds.

"Well, it could be important, in the context of Josh. And why he did what he did," Reagan points out.

Ella purses her lips. "I suppose that's true."

"The police will sort it out, I guess," Reagan says.

The reality settles back in.

Ted and Brady are down at the station.

Neither Ella nor Reagan have any idea how that's playing out.

There's a loud thud and both of them sit up straight.

The lights flicker on.

"Oh, thank goodness," Reagan says, and she excuses herself to go plug in her phone.

Ella sits with her head in her hands, struggling to interpret what Reagan said. Hoping that Reagan hasn't remembered anything incriminating. Hoping that this weekend will wrap up without anyone else getting hurt. And wondering how much time she has before it all blows up in her face.

THIRTY-TWO
REAGAN

I'm shaking like a leaf.

Somehow, Ella knows that I saw something that night.

Why did I ask if she thought Lanie was seeing someone senior year? That was a stupid thing to say. I forgot myself for a moment, and I can only hope she doesn't suspect that I've remembered some of what I saw and heard that night.

Right now, what I have recalled isn't directly incriminating to Ella or to Ted. All I know is that Lanie was pregnant. And she didn't want to hook up with Josh because of it. But whatever it was, it's clear to me that it's a threat to Ella.

My plan is to leave now. Tonight. Before any more memories surface, now that the storm is starting to die down. I don't have a great poker face, and with no internet or TV or anything to distract us, it's hard to avoid Ella and her penetrating stares. Not to mention her interrogations, disguised as small talk.

The rain has let up, and I'll take my chances on the roads. I can't stay here with her all night. Who knows what she might do with her back against the wall? I'm a bad liar, and I fear she can see right through me. I may get stuck in the mud, but if I take enough food and water, I can make it one night. Search and rescue teams are out. I think I'm safer alone.

Plugging in my phone, I try to stay hopeful. I think of Danny and imagine holding him in my arms and drinking in his sweet baby scent. Trying to stay positive, I picture a typical evening at home. Matt and me on the sofa, scrolling through Netflix for something to watch. I'll never complain about being bored again. All I want is to be home. Safe. With my family.

Family is everything.

For me.

But also for Ella.

I can't let myself forget who I'm up against.

Throwing my things in my bag in preparation for my exit, I try to stay quiet. I need to let my phone charge a bit before I take off. For some reason, I don't want to let on that I'm planning to leave until the last possible minute. I feel like Ella might protest or try to talk me out of it.

Or worse.

Clanking sounds in the kitchen tell me that Ella's cleaning up from our meal, so I can stall a bit longer. My bags are packed but I'm trying to get my phone charged up. I plugged it in last night but the socket is worn, so it fell out a little, to the point where there wasn't enough contact for it to charge, and I don't have much battery left.

I had it turned off, since I can't get any bars in my room, ironically, to save battery, so I didn't notice until I went to call Matt. But I'll be able to charge it in the car, so what I have should hold me over until I get down the mountain.

As I prepare to exit my room, I hear a vehicle drive up. It sounds like a truck.

I peek out my window and see a Hummer SUV, its bright headlights shining at me. I can't see who is in the car, but I know who it is because I know the vehicle.

Ella's parents.

I suppose that could be good. Maybe they know something and are here to update us. And it's a good sign that they made it here. Of course, my Camry is no match for a Hummer in hurricane aftermath conditions. But at least I know the road is open.

Hanging back, I wait for her parents to enter the cabin. The less time I spend alone with Ella, the better. The screen door bangs shut, but I don't hear anyone talking in the living room. I hear voices outside, but I can't see anyone because the car is turned off.

"What are you doing here?" Ella says.

"I came to explain," a man's voice replies.

It's Ella's father.

Ella's father's voice.

It hits me like a lightning bolt.

I hear the voice outside my window, ten years ago.

Lanie, be reasonable.

Ella's father.

It's the same voice.

Lanie was sleeping with Ella's father?

More memories come rushing back to me, although I wish they wouldn't. These are fuzzier, from when I was still on ecstasy and drunk off my ass.

A man grabs me and whips me around.

I scream.

I see a face now. I think?

It's Rob Parker. Is it?

Or am I trying to force myself to make a connection that's not there?

We have some unfinished business, a voice says.

My stomach sinks now, as I grasp the implication.

But it all makes sense. Horrible, perfect sense.

Lanie was pregnant with Rob Parker's child.

He was here that night.

He knows I saw him ten years ago, the night Lanie died.

He probably confused me with Lanie.

Josh knew something about this, too.

Josh is dead.

And Rob Parker is here now.

THERE'S no time to hesitate. As soon as they head into the house, I'll jump out the window and run for my life. The window is small, though, and it sticks. I try to shove it up, but can't get it all the way open, and I'll never fit through the space. The rainwater must have swelled the wood frame. I might have to break the glass. I weigh that against the option of playing it cool and simply telling Ella that I'm heading home.

Would they really try and stop me?

With Ted and Brady down at the station?

Because the thing is, my mind is still playing tricks on me. The only thing I'm sure of is the voice outside my window. I was sobering up by that time, and I know that it was Ella's father's voice that night. The other memory is fuzzy. The one with the face. Sort of like a dream.

It's quite possible that my mind filled in her father's face, trying to make sense of a bunch of random thoughts and memories. I'm not sure that really happened. Because if it had, he'd probably have tried harder to silence me over the years. But I feel like someone grabbed me. It's all so muddled.

I do remember coming into the living room the night I heard Lanie say she was pregnant, after I used the bathroom. And I told Ella about it. She said it was a dream. That I was still out of my mind. At the time, I believed her, but really, by that point, I'd sobered up quite a bit. But she doesn't know that, and she could think I don't remember it. So if I can play it cool and pretend I didn't remember her father's voice outside my window, I can probably slip out of here without a problem and get on with my life.

If I break the window, she'll know I'm on to her.

But if I don't, I might blow my only chance of getting out of here alive.

THIRTY-THREE
REAGAN

Ella and her father are still outside, so I can't try to break the window yet, but I think it's my best option. I look around to see if I can barricade the door, which will at least buy me some time if they hear the sound of glass shattering. There's a large oak dresser that looks very heavy, and I'm not sure if I can move it, and a small nightstand that won't do much of anything.

The dresser is about five feet from the door, up against the wall that sits perpendicular to the one housing the door and door frame. Even if I could use my weight to push the dresser in the general direction, I don't think I could turn it by myself.

Unless I take out the drawers.

Do I have time?

That's my best option, I decide.

So, I pull out the bottom one, but it catches.

Damn it.

I can't get it to release.

I need another plan.

Recalling a video I saw once about how to survive a mass shooting by barricading yourself inside a room, I double check that the door swings inward.

It does.

I'm in luck.

If I can find something to wedge under the door, that will do the trick, at least for a while. Scavenging through the closet, I find a cardboard shoebox with photos in it and dump them on the bed, hoping I can fashion something out of the cardboard.

But I'll also need something to break the window, and there's nothing I spot in this room that will work. Ella and her father have been outside for a pretty long time, and I don't have time to think about what that means. Instead, I use it to my advantage. Opening the bedroom door, I take a chance, bolt over to the fireplace, grab the poker, and dash back into my room.

Closing the door behind me, I force the cardboard box top into a wedge shape and jam it into the space between the floor and the bottom of the door. Then I put the nightstand in front of it, to give me a little added protection. Now all I need to do is wait until they come inside and make my move. An eerie calm has washed over me, like I'm detached from reality, but I know it's just a matter of time before it all hits me.

And then I start to have second thoughts.

Perhaps this is a crazy move, and I'm overreacting. Maybe playing along is the right thing to do.

But then I picture Lanie, down in that ravine, and I recommit to my plan.

I'm not ending up like her.

Then something totally unexpected happens.

I hear the Hummer start up and drive away.

Is her father leaving?

Where would he be going?

Maybe he's fleeing the country or something. And if he is, it's none of my concern. I need to focus on getting out of here alive. That also means it's just me and Ella now, which is better for me. And I've got the fireplace poker as a weapon.

"Reagan?" she calls out.

Crap, she's in the house already.

Trying to sound calm and collected, I reply. "I'll just be a minute. I'm getting changed."

And then I make my move.

Holding the poker like a baseball bat, I swing at the window. It shatters, but chunks of glass still stick to the sides of the wooden window frame.

"What are you doing in there, Reagan?" Ella cries out. "Are you okay? Did you fall?"

She tries to open the door and my makeshift barricade holds for now. But the cardboard wedge is flimsy, and I don't have much time. My phone is in my pocket, along with my car keys. I wrap a shirt around each hand to protect me from the glass.

With the poker, I strike at the sharp shards of glass and watch them fall to the ground outside. Then I hoist myself up and start to climb out the window.

Ella bangs on the door, and can almost see that cardboard wedge popping out and the door swinging open. I need to move fast, but I also need to be careful. I can't go too fast or I'll cut myself.

"Reagan! What the hell are you doing? Let me explain," Ella pleads.

Yeah, right. Let you explain how you and your family murdered two people and then tried to cover it up because your father was sleeping with your best friend?

I might not have all the answers yet, but I have enough of them to know that these people are killers. I'm going straight to the police and telling them everything.

I'm almost out the window, with one leg in and one leg out, straddling it. But when I pull my second leg through, I lose my balance and my upper thigh scrapes the top of the frame.

Agggghhh.

A piece of glass rips through my jeans and into the top of my leg. A searing pain nearly causes me to pass out. My stomach roils and bile rises in my throat. I start to feel the blood soak the denim of my pants leg, and soon I'm sure it will be dripping down my leg. I can't lose it, though. I suppress the urge to cry out. She can't know that I'm injured.

Sprinting toward my car, as much as I can in the thick mud, I'm confident I can make it. Ella hasn't figured out yet that I'm outside, but she will soon. I can't think about whether or not I'll get stuck trying to pull out of the muddy driveway.

Ella pokes her head out the bedroom window and calls out to me. "Reagan! What are you doing? We need to talk!"

I race over and try to open the car door. It's locked, although I don't remember locking it. It's a habit, I guess. Patting my jeans pocket, my stomach sinks.

My keys!

They must've fallen out when I climbed out the window

and lost my balance. Ella is at the front door now. I've got my phone and the fireplace poker, and now I've only got one move.

I've got the jump on her. "Stay back, Ella!" I scream, shaking the fire poker at her.

"Have you lost your mind?" she cries out.

Tossing the poker on the ground, I spin around and run for my life, bolting into the woods with the muck and the wet and the darkness. I know that this is an insane move, but I keep running and running and as I do, I hear Ella shouting to me. Over and over and over.

"Reagan! Stop! I can explain."

Not a chance in hell.

She's following me

Ella's a survivor.

But so am I.

I kind of wish I hadn't tossed my only weapon, but the forest is thick with foliage and it would be harder to maneuver through the gnarled tree trunks and sharp branches with it in my hand. Not stopping to look behind me, I keep going, forging ahead. Until her cries get softer and softer and I can't breathe because the panic hits me and the pain in my leg begs for my attention.

Stopping to catch my breath, I realize two things:

Ella isn't shouting at me anymore.

I'm only wearing one shoe.

THIRTY-FOUR
ELLA

Ella's throat feels like sandpaper from yelling to Reagan, and she finally gives up and turns back to the cabin. Upon returning inside, she sits on the sofa, hangs her head in her hands, and sobs. This is a luxury she rarely affords herself, and she knows this is the last thing she should be doing. But it's been a long time coming, and it's hitting her like a tidal wave.

Her sobs are devoid of sound, because the spasms are so strong; she struggles to even breathe, and for a moment, it feels as if she might hyperventilate. Letting the hysteria wash over her, the release comes in waves. She's able to steady herself for a time, but then it erupts again. After she's spent, she stares into space, knowing she needs to take action, but still frozen to her spot on the sofa.

Right now, nothing is real. Right now, she's at her family's camp in the Adirondacks where they laughed and played games and let their hair down. A place of innocence and lightness, where some of her happiest memories of childhood were formed.

Before it all came crashing down.

Ella's taken back to that moment in the cabin ten years ago, when the whole sordid truth revealed itself before her eyes. The depth of Lanie's betrayal. The summer before, when Ella's father offered Lanie an internship, Ella remembers feeling a little pang of trepidation in the pit of her stomach. Something didn't sit right with her, but she'd brushed it off. Told herself she was reading too much into their stolen glances and her father's wandering eye.

When Lanie came home with Ella for that first Thanksgiving freshman year, Ella's mother took her in like a second daughter. Her father seemed uncurious, even bothered by Lanie's presence in the house. But over the weekend, he took a liking to Lanie, seeming to see in her something of himself.

Her father is self-made. Driven. And Ella remembers some tense conversations between her parents revolving around their child-rearing philosophies as she was growing up, with her father concerned that they were spoiling Ella and her brother. That they wouldn't have the hunger required to make it in a cutthroat world if they had everything handed to them on a silver platter. Ella's mother grew up with money, but her father didn't. Perhaps that's why he took such a liking to Ted, and why Ella picked a man like Ted to begin with. Ted had that same hunger, like her father. They'd both do whatever it took to get ahead.

What a cliché.

Marrying a guy like your father.

Why hadn't she seen it until now?

Over time, her father took an interest in Lanie and her

career. But to Ella, it felt like more than simply a mentorship. Her mother seemed oblivious, but apparently, she wasn't. She was playing the long game.

When Lanie told Ella the truth that night, ten years ago, that she was pregnant with her father's child and planning to have the baby, Ella couldn't bear to burden her mother, preferring to leave her in blissful ignorance.

Instead, she called her brother Ben, and he suggested that it was a shakedown. That perhaps Lanie was just making it up or threatening to have the baby to get some kind of payoff, and that perhaps Ella should offer Lanie a nice sum of money to make the problem go away. Ben never liked Lanie, maybe because she brushed off his mild flirtations, preferring someone a bit more mature, it seems. The whole affair turns Ella's stomach.

She knows Reagan heard part of that conversation with her brother ten years ago.

Is that what Reagan remembered that caused her to freak out?

Is that what made her bolt into the woods?

Or was it something more?

Did Reagan perhaps overhear Ella's own conversation with Lanie?

Of course, Lanie didn't take the payoff. "You think this is about money? You're sick. All of you," Lanie scoffed.

"*I'm* sick? You slept with my *father*, Lanie. How could you? How could you do that to me?" Ella said.

"I didn't do anything to you. This isn't about you, Ella. For once, try and think of someone other than yourself. He came on to me. He was my boss. I'm the victim here. Why can't you see that?"

Ella turned from Lanie so she wouldn't have to look her in the eye. She made a fair point. And it was all so humiliating. For Ella. For all of them. And people would likely sympathize with Lanie over Ella's dad. But family is family, and there was never a question as to whose side Ella was on.

Perhaps emboldened by Ella's prolonged silence, Lanie continued. "You Parkers all stick together, right? Well, now I'm one of you. And so is this baby. And you're not getting out of this with a payoff. You're all stuck with me now. And if you don't like it, you can blame your damn father."

As if that wasn't bad enough, Lanie had to go and tell Josh about the pregnancy, and that their family offered her a payoff, giving him ammunition to use to his advantage.

And Josh.

What about him?

Well, on some level, one could say he got what he deserved. Blackmail is a crime. Josh was a criminal. An opportunist. But Ella still feels guilty about his death. And confused about it, too. Her father said he was going to talk some sense into him, not murder him. Perhaps there's another explanation. Maybe Josh really did feel guilty for profiting from Lanie's death.

But guilty enough to shoot himself in the head?

Pulling herself together, Ella dries her eyes, grabs her car keys, and sets out to find Reagan.

Before it's too late for her, too.

THIRTY-FIVE
REAGAN

I have no idea where I am, aside from the fact that I'm headed down the mountain. It's started to rain again, and I'm soaking wet, shivering and sweating at the same time, which I didn't know was possible. My right sneaker must have gotten stuck in the mud, and I'm tempted to try and go back for it.

But I have no idea how long it's been gone, so it's probably a waste of time. It was dusk when I started into the woods, but now it's full on night time, and I don't know how long the flashlight on my phone will last. I need to keep moving, and I can't do this in the dark. I can only hope the battery holds out.

A numbness has washed over me. But I forge ahead, like a zombie. Yes, that's what I feel like. A zombie. I probably look like one, too. Maybe I'm in shock. My leg is throbbing, though, so probably not. When you're in shock, you're not supposed to feel pain; at least that's what I've heard. The bleeding seems to have stopped, thankfully. I just need to keep going.

Down the mountain.

To the road, where I can wave someone down.

Or to a spot where I can get cell service.

I know we're about a thousand feet or so up the mountain, but I have to wind around, so it will be a little longer than that, maybe three thousand feet? Or more? I struggle to recall how many feet are in a mile. Five thousand something? So, it shouldn't be more than a few miles down to the road, even if I'm zig-zagging. Without my shoe, though, it's slow going. I have on thick socks, which is better than nothing, but if I step on something sharp, I'm toast.

The numbness wears off and I start to feel sick to my stomach. Struggling with a wave of panic that rises up, threatening to get my heart racing and sap my strength, I try to remember to breathe.

In for four, hold for seven, out for eight.

My lack of supplies and the darkness closing in is freaking me out. I don't have any water, and I'm hoping that won't be a problem. Then a thought crosses my mind. Something I was told at one point in my life. I can't recall who told me. I think I learned it in a first aid class I had to take when I worked as a camp counselor. The rule of three, regarding survival.

Three minutes without air.

Three days without water.

Three weeks without food.

Even if it feels as if I'm thirsting to death, I'm not. I have three days before I'll need to worry about it. But I lost some blood.

Doesn't that make it worse?
I fight not to lose it.
You're safe.
You will get home to Danny and Matt.
To your boring little life in front of the TV, searching for a Netflix series to binge.

AFTER ABOUT TWENTY minutes of slogging through the muck and ducking dangling tree branches that poke out like daggers in the night, hoping I don't lose another shoe or heaven forbid, an eye, I stop to pull my phone out of my pocket and check. Still no service.

Ella said the service cuts in and out, even in the woods. But if the cell tower is still out, I may be out of luck even if I get down to the road. I wonder if GPS could even track me at this point. I have no idea where I am, or if anyone could even find me. I have no choice but to soldier on. If I get to the road, I can flag a car down.

But I'm so tired. And wet. And cold. Looking down, I notice that my leg is bleeding again, but not nearly as much as before. Perhaps I'm losing more blood than I realize and that's sapping my strength. I wipe the sweat from my brow and see that it's tinged red. I must have cut my forehead on a branch. I'm so damn tired. Maybe I should sit for a bit.

No. I can't do that. Picturing my son and the promise I made to the universe, I press on. And as luck would have it, I spot a path on my right and perk up.

A path.

This means it will go so much faster. I won't have to

chart my way through the dense forest. I can just put one foot in front of the other. Squinting in the distance, I see lights whooshing by. It's got to be cars. I'm close to the main road. I can do it.

One foot in front of the other.

Willing my blood to clot, I keep going.

One foot in front of the other.

Trying not to think about the fact that I'm bone tired.

One foot in front of the other.

Trying not to think about the fact that I have no idea what will happen when I finally find my way off this mountain and get back to safety.

Chances are, nobody knows what Rob Parker did except the Parkers, Josh, and Lanie. And Josh and Lanie are dead. It's the family's word against mine. My mother's words ring in my ears. *You're not the most reliable narrator, Reagan.*

But I can't worry about that now.

One foot in front of the other.

For Danny.

For my little bundle of joy.

For Matt, the love of my life.

I'll figure the rest of it out later.

FINALLY, I see a road in the near distance. I'm starting to fade, but it's so close. Gathering a last burst of strength, I run out toward the road. My knees are about to buckle, and the nausea is starting again.

A car is coming.

Just in time. I'm about to pass out.

I'm going to wave it down.

They're going to save me.

But my sock slips on the muddy shoulder as I reach the edge of it, and I go skidding into the road. My body seizes up to try and stop me, and I try to swing myself in the opposite direction, away from the road.

But I've got too much momentum.

The headlights blind me.

A terrible thud.

A crushing pain.

I go flying into the air.

And then it all goes black.

THIRTY-SIX
REAGAN

My eyes flutter open. The first face I see is Matt's, just like ten years ago, almost to the day. He's sleeping in a chair next to my hospital bed. Rather than wake him, I take in my surroundings and try to piece together what happened as I listen to the rhythmic beeping sound of the heart monitor telling me I'm still alive. It could have been worse.

There's a chart on the wall with the date and other instructions the nurses write on the whiteboard. I've been here overnight. No memory problems this time. I remember everything.

Lanie was pregnant.

With Rob Parker's child.

He killed Lanie to shut her up.

I fled the house, to get away from them because it all came rushing back to me in a flash when I heard him outside my window—just like my therapist said it might.

But then a terrifying thought occurs to me.

What if I'm wrong?

Or what if I'm right, but nobody believes me?
I have no proof to offer the police.

Nothing her father said today—or yesterday, I guess, as I seem to have lost a day—was incriminating. And with my reputation and my drug-induced state ten years ago, I hardly present as a reliable witness, especially after I broke a window and fled into the forest in the aftermath of a hurricane like a crazy person.

What if they try to paint me as unstable?
As an unfit mother?
And where is Danny?
Why is Matt here without him?

I long for my baby boy. To hold him against me and feel the weight of his little body in my arms.

What if I lose everything?

I should have kept my mouth shut. Left it alone. Lanie's not my problem. She's not my responsibility. Danny is my responsibility, and I can only hope they don't try to make me out as the crazy one. I *am* my own worst enemy, it seems. I chuckle at this thought and realize that I must be medicated.

In fact, I've been so preoccupied with these debilitating ruminations, I've hardly had a moment to take inventory of my body. I was hit by a car. Common sense tells me I shouldn't try to move until I know what I'm dealing with.

There's a dull ache in my right leg and my head is pounding. I'm sure I'm on some strong pain meds or it would be a whole lot worse. I pull my head up slightly and I'm glad to feel it rise. My neck seems to work. I can wiggle my toes. But I see that my right leg is in a cast, which pokes out from under the blanket. Yellow hospital socks cover my feet.

Matt's eyes open and he places his hand on mine.

"Hey," he says. "How long have you been up?"

"Just a few minutes," I say.

"You need the nurse?"

"I don't think so. I'd like some water, though. I'm thirsty. Can I have some water?"

"Yeah," he says.

Matt grabs the small pitcher of water on my nightstand and brings the straw to my lips. I take a cautious sip, wondering how it will feel going down because I realize that my throat is sore. It feels heavenly, so I take another and then another.

"The ice melted. I can get more," he says. "If it's not cold enough."

"It's fine," I say. "Why is my throat sore?"

"You had surgery on your right leg. It took the impact from the car. It was pretty badly broken. I think they put a tube down your throat during surgery, so that's probably why it's sore."

My stomach lurches. What if I lose my mobility? What if I can never walk again?

"Am I going to be okay?" I ask, not sure if I want to hear the answer.

"Yeah," he says. "You got lucky. Seems you jumped out of the way at the last second and the car only clipped you. Once the break and your other lacerations heal, you should be good. You may need some physical therapy, but the doctor says you should come back from it just fine."

Struggling to read his expression, I fear the worst. That everyone views this as another crazy Reagan episode. And I struggle to find a way to explain my behavior that doesn't land me in a mental institution.

What kind of crazy person takes off in the aftermath of a hurricane and hurls themselves in front of a moving vehicle? That's how this will play out, I'm sure of it. They might even think I tried to kill myself.

I know what I heard ten years ago, though.

Lanie was pregnant.

I'm sure of that much.

But was it really Ella's father's voice I heard?

Was it his face I saw?

Or did my mind try to fill in the gaps for me?

I start to second guess myself and my decision to go to the police and tell them everything. Maybe the face I saw was simply a figure of my imagination, a way for my mind to try and make sense of a bunch of random thoughts. The detectives can figure out what really happened to Lanie and Josh. It's not my problem. They are the experts. I don't need to be a hero.

Why isn't my husband saying anything?

Finally, Matt speaks. "A lot has happened, Reagan. But I don't want to overwhelm you."

"Overwhelm me?" I reply.

"The news is a little shocking. But then I feel like you might already have an inkling about it. But you've been through so much. I'm not sure if this is the right time to..."

My eyes widen, to the extent that they can, being dulled by the morphine, or whatever is dripping into my veins. "Just tell me, Matt. Please. It can't be any worse than what I'm imagining."

"Rob Parker's been arrested," he says. "For the murders of Lanie Martin and Josh Tanner."

Taking a deep breath, I let the news sink in. It's a relief, for sure, but there's another emotion lurking beneath it. I'm not sure what it is yet, so I sit with it for a bit and let it stew. Something bordering on anger. Maybe indignation, for the way I've been treated. For the fact that people patronize me and don't give me the benefit of the doubt.

Because, all along, I was right.

"Reagan? Did you hear me?"

"I heard you," I say. "I knew it was him. That's why I ran."

"How did you know?" he asks.

"It's a long story."

"We have time," he says.

So I tell him my story.

And for once, someone really listens.

WE'RE ABOUT FINISHED when an officer enters.

It's Officer Branson, the menacing one from the cabin.

I look over at Matt.

His eyes widen and his pupils seem to enlarge.

Does Matt think I'm in some kind of trouble?

Or does Branson just have that effect on people?

"Hello, Ms. Hansen. I'd like to have a chat. Are you up for it?" he asks.

Matt's jaw tightens.

He springs to my defense. "My wife's been through a lot."

"No, I'm okay," I say. "I want to tell you what I know, while it's fresh in my mind."

Officer Branson asks my husband to leave the room.

Then he reiterates what Matt told me. Rob Parker confessed to Lanie's murder, sort of. He claims it was an accident. But he swears he didn't kill Josh Tanner and try to make it look like a suicide.

Branson asks me why I ran.

I tell him about my memory returning, about hearing Ella's father's voice, and that I figured out Rob Parker was the father of Lanie's child. He doesn't seem too interested in that weekend ten years ago. He starts asking me questions about Josh.

What was his state of mind before he went for the run?
Did we have an altercation?

My stomach tenses, but I'm not surprised that he knows about our argument. Brady probably told him, trying to throw suspicion toward me and away from himself. It's fine. I have an alibi for the time Josh was out. He doesn't.

I explain to Branson about Josh and our history. And that Josh revealed to me that he was in love with Lanie. I tell the officer that Josh seemed broken up about Lanie's death, and that he obviously cared about her more than any of us knew.

And I can only hope that the rest of us did the same.

Because we all had motive to kill Josh Tanner and make it look like a suicide.

It seems very risky, though, and I can tell Branson thinks so, too. He seems to want to believe it was a suicide. The questions he's asking are leading me in that direction. So I give him what he seems to want. Josh was grief-stricken. I point out that he even texted everyone that he needed some time alone, and couldn't even bring himself to go to the service.

Branson nods. "We'll be in touch as the investigation develops," he says.

And he goes on his way.

When Matt returns, he chastises me for talking to the police without an attorney present.

"You never do that, Reagan," he says. "That's criminal defense one-oh-one."

"I have nothing to hide," I say.

"It doesn't matter. Innocent people get charged and convicted all the time, and with your history with Josh..."

"What are you driving at?" I ask.

"Nothing, babe. Just trying to protect you, that's all."

I smile, but I wonder.

Does my husband think I might incriminate myself?

Does he think I may have done something to Josh?

Or is this just Matt being a cautious guy?

Matt's an insurance guy, I remind myself. He was an actuary, before he moved up to vice president, the person at the company who calculates risk for a living. So, it's natural that he'd think like this. That's the way his mind works. And he's right. If there is a next time, I'll bring an attorney.

But somehow, I don't think there will be.

THIRTY-SEVEN
ELLA

It's the end of one of the most challenging days of Ella's life, but not the worst one. The worst day of her life was when she figured out the truth about what really happened to Lanie Martin ten years ago.

For nearly a year after that horrific morning, Ella had her suspicions, but she didn't know for sure that someone had pushed Lanie that night. In fact, even when she pieced it all together, she didn't know for certain what actually transpired until her father confessed yesterday.

At first, she believed Lanie's death was an accident. At least that's what she told herself, although she knew it was a lie that Lanie was wasted. But Lanie was upset, and Ella felt a little guilty that she hadn't been more supportive. Lanie was right. Ella shouldn't have blamed her. Her father was Lanie's superior. A grown man, twice her age. A married man, with a family. Even if Lanie had been a willing participant, it was her father who was more in the wrong. But family is family, so she stuffed it all down and swallowed it whole.

It crossed Ella's mind that day that her brother Ben might have taken action, but later, it became clear that he wasn't at the camp that night. His social media showed that he'd been four hours away, on a getaway with his girlfriend. But a year or so after that, Ben finally confessed to Ella that he'd called their father that night to warn him. And that's when Ella began to suspect that her father had done something to Lanie.

Her mother was a wreck for months after Lanie's death, and she hardly talked to her father during that time. Ella assumed that her mother knew about the affair. And if her mother had known that her father went up to the camp that night, she'd decided to stay quiet about it, at least in the short term.

By that time, Josh was already blackmailing the family, and they were all sworn to secrecy. If it came out about Lanie's pregnancy, their entire lives could be derailed, especially given the fact that the death happened on their property.

Ted knew everything, and he convinced Ella that it was in their best interest to keep quiet about it. None of them knew for sure that her father had been there that night, but with the payoffs to Josh, well, everyone knew how it would look. Nobody could know about Lanie's pregnancy.

And Reagan knew.

That's why Ella planned the weekend gathering in the first place. Because Reagan was starting to remember things about that night, Matt said, and if she remembered something about the pregnancy, it could be dangerous for Ella's family—and for Reagan. And Ella's father and Ted also figured it would be a good opportunity for them to "talk some sense" into Josh, and get him to stop his shakedown, once and for all.

It must have gotten to her mother over the weekend, at Lanie's memorial service, especially after Josh went missing and was found dead.

Because Ella's mother went to the police and told them she thought her husband might have killed Josh Tanner. She disclosed to them that Josh had been blackmailing them for the last ten years. She told them about her husband's affair years ago and about Lanie Martin's pregnancy. She revealed nothing regarding her suspicions about Lanie's death and simply let them put the pieces together.

Her mother admitted to the police she'd known about the affair, but claimed that she and her husband had gotten past it. But she informed them that her husband was fed up with Josh Tanner and that he told his wife that he would put an end to his blackmail scheme this weekend, once and for all.

When the police arrested Ella's father, he confessed that he'd gone to the camp ten years ago, had an argument with Lanie Martin about the baby, and caused her to fall to her death—accidentally. He said he was talking to her outside the cabin, but she ran off into the woods. And when he caught up with her, well, things got a little out of hand. He admitted that they'd argued even more in the woods. He offered her more money, and she slapped him in the face. He grabbed her by the wrist, but she pulled away from him. She ran from him, and she fell.

But he swears up and down he had nothing to do with Josh Tanner's death. He doesn't own a gun, he told them. He had planned on talking to Josh that weekend, he said, which is why they came up to the camp. But by that time, Josh was on his run or hike or whatever, so he didn't get a chance to have that talk with him. They were planning on telling Josh they would go to the police if he didn't stop, figuring there was no evidence linking him to Lanie's death. Ted was supposed to handle it for him, and Ella shudders to think what that could mean. And for the last hour, Ella's been grilling Ted about it.

Because Ted hated Josh.

"I swear to you, Ella. I had nothing to do with Josh's death. I went to look for him. Like your father wanted. To tell Josh once and for all that it was over. Blackmail's a crime, so we were planning to threaten to turn him in. There was nothing linking your father to Lanie's death, at least there wasn't at the time. We figured Josh would see he had more to lose than your father did. He would surely be convicted for the blackmail. We had all the evidence. And he had no proof your father was there that night. Having an affair isn't a crime."

"But why did my mother tell the police she thought my dad killed Josh?"

Ella's mother has not been returning her phone calls, and Ella hasn't been allowed to see her father yet, so everything she knows is from Ted, who was at the police station when this all went down. Her father's attorney briefed Ted and guided him through his interview with the police. But even Ted doesn't know everything, which is apparently typical in a homicide investigation.

Ted shrugs. "Maybe she thought he did it. He was pissed off. Fed up with Josh."

Ella lets out a huff.

"Maybe he *did* do it, Ella," Ted says.

"That makes no sense," Ella replies. "My mother was with him the whole time, wasn't she?"

"No," Ted says. "Your father went to the store for flashlight batteries, remember?"

Ella's hand goes to her forehead. "You're right."

"I'm not out of the woods on this, either, Ella. I have the receipts from the store and the GPS on my car, which I think should clear me when they get an official time of death. But until then, I'll be sweating bullets. I need a lawyer, and not one who's connected in any way to your parents."

"What about Brady? Was he cleared?"

"No idea," Ted says. "They didn't let us talk to each other. He lawyered up."

Ella places her hand on his. "I'm sorry, Ted. About all of it."

"It's not your fault. But we have to protect ourselves and our children. Your father's already going down for one murder, so maybe you can talk him into...taking one for the team here."

"You want him to confess to a murder he didn't do?" Ella asks.

"We don't know that he didn't do it," Ted offers. "Your father's not stupid. He knows there's a difference between involuntary manslaughter and a first-degree murder charge. If he killed Josh, he wouldn't admit it to the police. He'll take his chances at trial."

"Oh, come on, Ted. I mean, one accident I can see. But staging a suicide?"

Ted shrugs. "Maybe Josh really did kill himself," he says. "Maybe it's that simple. He obviously cared about Lanie. And to profit off of her death instead of going to the cops about what he knew? It's pretty sickening. It could have gotten to him. You know how broken up he was that weekend, when she died. And he sent those text messages," he points out.

Ella wants to believe this. With all her heart, she does. Even though she knows for a fact that Josh has a Samsung phone and uses fingerprint ID to open it. The killer could have sent those texts after he was dead. Still, she forces all the suspicion—about her husband, her father, her brother, and even her mother—deep down where it can never surface again.

"You're right," she says to Ted. "Maybe it is that simple. Josh killed himself, out of guilt."

That is what Ella told the police when she was questioned. Josh was beside himself. The guilt and remorse seemed to be eating him alive.

She's not sure if they believed her, with her father in the hot seat. But it's the narrative she plans to stick with, to preserve what's left and come out of this with the least amount of damage.

Lanie will get justice, and Josh, well, perhaps he got what he deserved, whether by his own hand or another. But like her mother, Ella needs to protect her family. It's clear to Ella that her mother waited this long to turn her father in for a reason. Because she needed to make sure that her children were protected. That all of this wouldn't land back on them and ruin their chances in life. Her mother must have been furious with her father. Hurt. Confused. But she stuffed it all down and played the long game.

And so will Ella.

THIRTY-EIGHT
REAGAN

"How are you feeling?" the nurse asks.

Her name is Amy, and she's good at her job.

"I'm okay," I say.

And this time, I mean it. For the first time in ages, I trust myself. I trust my own judgement. It's a terrible burden to live without that assurance. To constantly be in doubt about your own perceptions. It feeds on itself, because once you start second-guessing yourself, it only gets worse. Then you start to ruminate and before too long, you can't even make a simple decision on your own.

I'm not exactly cured, but at least now I'm aware of the vicious cycle I've been stuck inside. As I fled the cabin and made my way to the road, the fear that nobody would believe me about the Parkers was equal to or greater in measure to the fear of them catching up with me.

Anticipating the humiliation that would consume me.

Feeling the knife twist in my gut.

It's almost worse than death. I mean, what's it all worth if you can't feel good about yourself? If those around you are constantly second-guessing your every move?

That's no way to live.

Matt went to get Danny from my mom, who's just arrived. I can only have two visitors at the same time, and apparently, an infant is a visitor.

Amy's busy, but not too busy to stop and talk to me. She pats my hand and assures me that I'll regain the mobility in my leg, before I even ask her about it, as if she's anticipating my fears before I can even articulate them.

She asks where my husband went, and I tell her about my baby boy.

"Oh, you must be excited to see him," she says with a warm smile. "I don't have kids yet. Soon, though, hopefully. I've been pretty busy with school and my job, but I'm not getting any younger."

She's different from the doctor, who's all business. In and out in a flash. Amy takes time to give a personal touch, but not in a prodding way, like a therapist. Like she's actually trying to connect with my humanity.

Amy has dark hair tied back in a high ponytail and pale skin indicative of long shifts under florescent lights. She looks about my age. I wonder if she always wanted to be a nurse.

"How long have you been a nurse?" I ask.

"About five years," she says. "I went back for a second bachelor's in nursing, after floundering for a while with a sociology degree. I decided on that after my grandmother got sick and I spent a lot of time with her in a rehab center."

"Do you like it?" I ask.

She flashes me a knowing smile and rolls her eyes.

What's she supposed to say? I mean, you can't tell your patient that you hate your job.

Amy sighs. "It's good for now. I want to be a psychiatric nurse practitioner. I've just applied to a few programs. I'd like to have more one-on-one time with patients, and not be so rushed all the time. And I'm interested in mental health. But yeah, I like it." She explains a bit about what the career she's shooting for entails. Then tells me she needs to get going.

A few minutes later, my mother comes in with Danny. I wasn't expecting her, and I'm not really in the mood to visit with anyone. I just want to hold Danny and be alone with him, and I want to tell her that.

But I don't.

"Hi, honey," she says.

I reach for Danny and she places him in my arms. I hug him close and feel the warmth of his little body. I swear he feels a tad bulkier than he did a few days ago. He's growing so fast now. Has it only been three days since I've seen him? It feels like so much longer. And I remember the promise I made to my little boy. Looking into his eyes, he gives me an ear-to-ear grin that tells me he's home now, in his mama's arms.

I tickle him. "I've missed you, little man."

Danny giggles.

My heart melts.

Then I remember that my mother is standing by my bedside. And suddenly I see her in my mind's eye, hugging me close, when I was just an infant. Vowing to protect me. And in a sort of epiphany, I understand her on a different level.

My mom's not perfect, that's for sure. But all of her hovering and intervening and second-guessing was done out of love, of that much I'm certain. Because if I'm being honest with myself, I wasn't the easiest kid to raise.

She bats back the tears starting to pool in her eyes. "You're a great mom, Reagan," she says. "And I'm proud of you."

"Sit, Mom," I say, suddenly happy for the company.

Matt has filled her in on the basics, but she asks me for more detail.

When did I suspect something was wrong?

How did I know to run?

"I didn't know for sure," I say.

"Well, turns out you have good instincts. Motherhood can do that to you. It changes a woman. Carrying another life inside. The maternal instinct. It's real."

I know what she means, but I'm tired, and I want to rest.

"I'm sorry, Reagan. I'm sorry that I doubted you and for, well, everything."

"I know, Mom. I'm sorry too. But I'm tired. Maybe we can do this another time."

"Sure, honey," she says. "I'm tired too. Danny's a handful. Oh, don't get me wrong. I love him to death. But two days in a row really wears me out."

Did I hear her right?

"Two days?" I ask.

"Yes. I started watching him yesterday, and I decided to stay over rather than drive home in the bad weather. Matt had to go into work for a while. Something about the hurricane and all the claims that were being filed. Thank goodness I did, because he got the phone call about you in the middle of the night."

That makes sense, I guess.

But I'm still tired. Not quite firing on all cylinders. I'm likely getting discharged today, so I may as well catch a little more sleep while I still have people waiting on me hand and foot.

So I give Danny to my mom.

We say our goodbyes.

Funny. Matt didn't say anything about my mom staying over at the house last night, or coming over and watching Danny all day on Saturday.

And I drift off.

THIRTY-NINE
ELLA

Ella waits with her mother at her parents' home, for word of her father's case. Ted has gone back to Saratoga Springs to take care of the kids. The attorney, a middle-aged firebrand named Denise Sherman, who looks like the human version of a Doberman Pincher, explained the process to them, and she's just left. There was no need for her to do that. Ella's already familiarized herself with the procedures, but she let the attorney walk them through it anyway.

Her father will be held in county jail until his arraignment, at which time his attorney will ask for bail. Sherman expects him to be released in the pre-trial phase, but there are no guarantees. He's confessed in the homicide of Lanie Martin, and she'll enter his plea of involuntary manslaughter when the time comes. The attorney is working her magic with the prosecution on a deal, but they have yet to make him an offer.

But Josh Tanner's death is another story. Ella's father swears he had nothing to do with Josh's death. He claims his wife jumped to conclusions and used the unfortunate incident as payback for his indiscretion with Lanie Martin years ago. Nobody knows yet how that will play out. The handwriting analysis of the suicide note was so far inconclusive, which the attorney told them is common these days. People don't write by hand as much anymore, so it's harder to tell for sure if the note was forged or authentic, at least to the degree that it would hold up in court.

If the police conclude it was a suicide, then Ella's father will probably get off with a pretty light sentence. If they conclude it was murder, he could spend the rest of his life in prison. Helen Parker seems indifferent to the outcome. She's planning to divorce her husband, she revealed to her daughter a few moments ago, after the attorney left. And with the prenup he signed, whatever the outcome of the criminal trial, he'll be penniless.

It's hard for Ella to believe that her mother just cooked all this up on the fly. There are a lot of questions she wants to ask, but she knows better than to ask most of them. She doesn't want to dig too much, because she's afraid of what she might find. Not that Ella blames her mother. It's her dad's fault for sleeping with Lanie to begin with. And on some level, she's impressed by her mother's moxie.

Who knew she had it in her?

Helen looks at her daughter and brushes a hand across her cheek. "Are you mad at me, honey? Husbands are replaceable. Fathers aren't. Have I made a mistake?"

"No, Mom. But why now? Why did you hold it in so long?"

"I needed to protect you. I was never sure what really

happened to Lanie. My children, I needed to protect the two of you if one of you had..."

"Oh, Mom. No, I'd never—"

"Your brother Ben found out about the affair months before he told you. He was angry. And I figured if he'd found out about the baby..."

"So you didn't know for sure? That Dad had been up at the camp that night?"

Helen shrugs. "You see what you want to see. Your father was away that weekend, at some business conference. I didn't check up on him at the time, but later I did." She sighs. "It was a lie. So many lies."

"But you knew about the affair? And the baby?"

"Yes," she says. "I overheard him on the phone with Lanie and he finally fessed up. He assured me he'd handle it with her. Offer her money, or something. And when I found out she died, I started to suspect that something happened that night. That she hadn't simply fallen. But then the blackmail began, and all I could think about was protecting you and Ben. Your futures. The statute of limitations has run out on all but the murder charge now, so we'll all be in the clear for whatever charges they could have thrown at us for withholding evidence."

"But what made you...do what you did, this weekend?" Ella asks.

"The guilt, I guess? That poor young woman. It wasn't her fault. She was practically a child. I cared about Lanie, and I'm not one of these women who blames the victim. But what could I do? I had no proof. And as I said, it could have been your brother. Or you, if I'm being honest. All that alcohol and anger. We never should have let you have that party. I just didn't know for sure what had happened. But after Josh was found dead, well, then it was clear to me what I needed to do."

Ella has her doubts about her mother's motives. "When you went to the police about Josh's death. Was that to get back at Dad? Or do you think he really did it? You can tell me, Mom."

"Your father told me that he would handle Josh. That the blackmail would come to an end, one way or another. So yes, I think he did it. I believe he staged the whole thing so it would look like Josh murdered Lanie, and he'd be in the clear. And that's what I told the police."

Ella's not sure if she believes her mother. It's possible that she saw an opportunity to stick it to her cheating husband and took it. In any event, it's not going to matter. Helen will testify to what her father said, and so will Ella. He was planning to neutralize Josh Tanner and stop the blackmail. The burden of proof is on the prosecution, and if the evidence isn't there, he'll be acquitted, or perhaps there won't even be enough for an indictment or a trial. But Ella also plans to drive home the point that Josh was remorseful. Guilt-ridden. Having this ruled a suicide is the best possible outcome all around.

"One other thing, Ella. Given your father's...predicament, I think Ted should take over as CEO of your father's business, with you and your brother as voting board members. This means either you will have to sell off the construction business, or you'll need to find someone to run it."

Ella's eyes widen. "Ted as CEO? No, Mom. Why not me?" Ella says.

Helen shrugs. "Is that something you even want to do? I thought you liked your downtime, and that you wanted to focus on the children."

"They're getting older," Ella says. And Ella absolutely wants to do this. She tries not to take offense at the fact that her mother was prepared to offer it to Ted.

"Ted's much better at construction, Mom. I have a business degree. Why wouldn't I want to do it?"

"If that's what you want. Of course. I'll have to talk to your brother about it. Make sure it doesn't ruffle any feathers."

Ella rolls her eyes. Her brother is a cardiologist. Why would it ruffle his feathers? She feels a little callous, scarfing up her father's lifetime achievement like it's a Black Friday sale. But then, he shouldn't have cheated. With her friend. Who was half his age.

Actions have consequences, and really, most everyone is getting what they deserve. Lanie. Josh. Her father. She needs to talk to Reagan, though. Explain it all to her. Tell her she would never have hurt her, and that she only gathered them there last weekend to protect her.

Ella thinks about the secret she's kept from Reagan all these years and wonders if she should come clean about that, too. It's an ace in the hole, of sorts. Something she should hold on to, just I case she needs it. She'll disclose it if it seems prudent, she decides.

For now, Ella tries to stay positive and strong. Her mother is angry, and rightly so. But Ella doesn't believe her father killed Josh, and a part of her hopes the evidence acquits him of that crime. He's her father, after all, but she's decided not to say anything like that to her mother, or the police. She'll let the evidence speak for itself.

But still, she shudders to think of what they might find when they start poking into what happened. They say it's a ghost gun. Untraceable. Ted's pretty street-smart. He'd be more likely to score one of those than her father.

And she doesn't say anything to her husband about her most pressing fear. That it very well might have been him. He despised Josh. If it's a choice between her father and Ted, there's no doubt in her mind where her loyalties lie. Hopefully, it won't come to that. If Ted did it, he'd never tell Ella. He'd throw the blame on her father, the one who started all this in the first place, and protect their children at all costs.

And so will she.

FORTY
REAGAN

It's been two weeks since the accident and I'm making progress. No more visits from the police. That seems to be fading into the distance. I'm off pain medication and can manage with Tylenol and ibuprofen. My cuts and bruises are healing up. Danny is sleeping through the night for the most part, and I'm feeling better each day.

Matt's been very busy at work, with all the flood damage claims, which made me nervous that perhaps the company might go under or cut salaries or that it would somehow affect our lives. Matt assures me the company is doing fine. The number of clients who filed claims was a small percentage of their overall business, he says, and homeowners isn't the only type of insurance they offer. It's all about diversification, according to Matt.

This put my mind at ease. Because I've been thinking a lot about my career and the fact that I'm not inspired at all by my present one. In order to make a change, Matt's career needs to be solid. Sure, my marketing job is convenient, and the pay is decent. I can work from home. It's not horrible. But I get no satisfaction out of it, and that's no way to go through life.

Matt doesn't exactly love his work, although he likes the money, so I've been reluctant to bring this up to him. He's the practical type, and he'd probably balk at the thought of my giving up a cushy situation to chase after an elusive goal like fulfillment. But perhaps I should give him the benefit of the doubt. He wants me to be happy, of that much I'm certain. Tonight, I'll bring it up and see what he thinks.

After my conversation with Amy the nurse, I looked into that career she said she wanted to pursue: psychiatric nurse practitioner. It's a long and tortured road to get there, but it seems like a doable, if challenging, long-term goal. I've had issues with therapists in the past, and although the one I have now is good, it took me a long time to find someone who didn't make me feel even worse about myself. I believe my problem is mostly chemical, and I'd like to help people like me.

Medical school isn't practical or even possible, to be realistic, so psychiatry is out of the question. I never wanted to be a psychologist and do talk therapy. This seems like a good fit for me. Psychiatric nurse practitioners can prescribe medication or counsel patients, or both. A stepping stone would be a mental health nurse, which is something I would like to do.

The first step would be a second bachelor's in nursing, which takes about two years. Well, actually, the first step would be the science prerequisites, which I could do online. We're talking a very long road to achieving this goal, but it's a road I'd be excited about, for once. For so long, I've just fallen into whatever came my way. It feels good to take charge of my life.

Right now, I'm waiting at a Starbucks for Ella, using the downtime to look up educational programs on my computer so when I talk to Matt, I'll have some idea of the cost and timeline. Ella and I haven't spoken since I climbed out the cabin window and ran for my life into the woods. She wanted to see me, and something about her coming to the house made me uncomfortable. Plus, it's good for me to get out. My mother dropped me off at the Starbucks closest to my house. I can't really drive yet. She's watching Danny.

It's midmorning, and Ella's driving down from Saratoga Springs. Weirdly, I'm looking forward to it rather than dreading it. Of course, I'm dying to know what's happening with her father, but I can't open with that. I expect she won't give up much about it, though. It's a delicate situation.

I'm seated at a table near the window, and I spot her walking toward the café. She waves, her blonde hair falling perfectly, skimming her navy blazer as it flips up at the ends, a politician-like smile on her face. Ella is a pro. At life. At everything. She rarely looks undone, and this time is no exception, even with her father facing a murder charge.

I look down at my outfit, a red sweater dress that flatters my curvy figure; pants are too difficult with this cast on my leg, so I've been wearing a lot of dresses. Matt likes it. He says I've got great legs, even with one of them in a cast. One consequence of my accident is that I've lost the baby weight, and I look damn good, if I do say so myself. Matt hasn't been able to keep his hands off me.

My hair finally got a cut and highlight, and there's a sparkle in my eyes that had been missing for the longest time.

I can see the difference in myself when I look in the mirror, even with a gash on my forehead that's still healing. I'm confident and grounded. Which might be the reason I'm looking forward to seeing Ella. I want to show off the new me.

I start to stand and greet her, but she protests.

Ella holds up her hand. "Don't get up. Let me go grab my latte. I ordered online."

She grabs her order, sits across from me, sips her coffee, and takes a good look at me. "Wow. You look...great. How are you feeling?"

"I'm getting there," I say. "How are you holding up with, well...everything?"

She sighs. "It's been hard, but I'm coping. You know me." She brushes a stray hair back from her face.

"Right," I say.

But do I?

"So," she says. "You're probably wondering why I called. And why I wanted to see you."

"Pretty much on the edge of my seat here, Ella." I smirk.

She offers me a hesitant smile. "I wanted to let you know that I brought you up to the camp to protect you."

My eyes widen. "Protect me? I nearly bled to death. I got hit by a car and almost died. Have you thought of joining the Secret Service?" I let out a chuckle.

Ella rolls her eyes. "Reagan, I'm trying to offer an olive branch here. I don't want to be enemies."

"I'm messing with you. A girl's gotta have a little fun. Go on. Enlighten me. About how you wanted to protect me." I hold her gaze, and she fidgets.

I made Ella Parker fidget.

She twirls a strand of hair, and then she speaks. "Okay. Look. I knew that you were starting to remember things from that night. Matt told me so. And I knew that you knew that Lanie was pregnant, ten years ago. You mentioned something about it to me when you came out of your bedroom to use the bathroom. I suggested it was a dream, to throw you off."

"I remember, Ella. Thanks for the gaslighting. Was that your way of protecting me? Making me think I was losing my mind?" Shaking my head, I offer her a smile. I don't want this getting too tense. She's a good person to have on my side, but I need to make her work for it.

Ella sighs. "Sorry, Reagan. I had to protect my family, too. You know how embarrassing that was for me? My father and Lanie? She told me about the baby that night. And she was defiant. She wanted to keep the baby. My family offered her a payoff but she wouldn't take it. And then she told Josh about the baby, and also about the payoff. And after we found her, after we knew she was dead, Josh started to blackmail us, threatening to go to the police about a motive."

My eyes nearly pop out of my head. "Josh knew that your father killed her? And he was blackmailing you? Profiting from Lanie's death?"

"No. He didn't know, but I'm sure he suspected. And with Lanie being pregnant, it wouldn't look good for my father or our family, especially with her dying on our property, if the affair came out. Josh milked us for years. My father was fed up with him. I was worried that if you remembered something about Lanie being pregnant, my father might get upset with you, too."

"Wow. I did not see that coming. Did you know that your father killed Lanie?"

"No," she says. "Of course not. But I had some suspicions about my brother. Because I called Ben that night and told him about Lanie's pregnancy, after she told me. The payoff was his idea. But I found out that Ben had an alibi, so then I was back to thinking it was an accident. About a year later, he told me that he'd called my father that night and told him. When my mother said Dad was out of town that weekend, well, it didn't look good. But no, I never knew anything for sure, not until he confessed."

"So that's who you were on the phone with that night," I say.

"Yes, when you came in the cabin. I guess you weren't that drunk, after all."

"Oh, no," I say. "I was pretty gone. It's taken ten years for me to piece the little bits I know together."

I explain to Ella how I remembered a voice outside the cabin ten years ago, but I couldn't place it. "But when I heard your father when he showed up that night..."

"It clicked." Ella nods. "And that's why you took off."

I shrug. "It wasn't my finest moment. I panicked. Or maybe not. I mean, I didn't know who to trust."

And I still don't.

I don't tell her about seeing her father's face in my vision, because I still don't know if that's real or a figment of my imagination. And then I ask what I really want to know.

Looking her square in the eye, I continue. "So, what's going on with your father's case?"

Ella reports what she knows, or what she's willing to tell me. "My father confessed, and he wants to plead guilty to involuntary manslaughter. It was an accident, he claims. He drove up late that night after the party died down. I have no idea where Lanie was all that time. And they got into an argument. She fell and..." Ella puts her head in her hands.

"You don't need to tell me any more," I say.

After a few minutes, she continues. "He left her there to die. But he swears he didn't kill Josh. His attorney is working on his defense. He's out on bail, for now. But my mom kicked him out of the house, so he's living up at the cabin."

I blow out a breath.

Wow.

"Do you believe him?" I ask.

"I want to," Ella says. "He's my dad. Of course, I want to believe him. But my mother is out for blood."

I have to hand it to Helen. I didn't think she had it in her.

"Your mother thinks your father did it?" I ask. "Staged Josh's suicide, and tried to pin Lanie's murder on him? That seems like a lot to plan."

"That's what she told the police," Ella replies.

"Maybe she's trying to protect someone else," I offer.

Ella's cold stare cuts through me like an icy dagger. "What are you driving at, Reagan?"

I swallow. "Nothing, Ella."

I need to walk it back, so I continue. "Maybe Josh killed himself. It could be that simple. He'd likely have been mortified if that came out. And if he was blackmailing your family and profiting from Lanie's death, if someone offed him, in my book, he deserved it. If you ask me, that Branson cop didn't seem too eager to pry much further into it."

Ella complicates my observation. "Well, it's really up to the DA, not the cop. They know my family, but the DA won't care who we are. They want a conviction. I wouldn't write this off too quickly. And there was no shortage of people up at the cabin who hated Josh. Brady fought with him that weekend, after all. And you did, too."

My jaw drops. "Me? I was with you the whole time."

"I'm merely pointing out the facts," she says.

"Has Brady been cleared?" I ask.

"I have no idea," she says.

I know the answer to this, because Brady and I have been keeping in touch, but I wanted to find out if Ella knew. He's been cleared, but he's just as perplexed as I am about what really happened to Josh. Both of us feel like it's probably someone in the Parker family, and neither of us is buying the suicide theory.

She can't have all the fun, so I go on the offensive. "What about Ted? Are you worried at all that they'll go after him? I'm not saying he did it, mind you. But he was out and about when Josh was out running. And he wasn't exactly fond of Josh."

Ella leans in. "Neither was Matt."

My brow furrows. "Matt? What's he got to do with it? He's never even been up to the cabin," I say.

But then I remember the phrase he used.

You're not near a stream, as I recall.

Does Ella know something I don't know?

"Hasn't he?" Ella replies.

My eyes narrow on her. "What are you getting at, Ella?" I ask.

She takes a deep breath and then continues. "Matt swore me to secrecy about this. But since we're coming clean, I'm going to tell you what I know. He came up to the cabin ten years ago to join the party, to surprise you. But then he saw you kissing Josh, and he changed his mind. I spotted him at the edge of the woods, watching you, and we caught each other's eye. I promised not to say anything to you. He was worried that you might have seen him, and he didn't want you to know he'd been there. I assured him that you were out of it, and that it meant nothing. But he was steaming mad. Not at you. But at Josh. I told him not to go. That he should talk to you. But he wanted to leave."

My stomach lurches.

All this time, Matt's known?

My head drops into my hands as I sit with this information.

Then I look up at Ella. "I planned to tell him right away. Explain to him that I only did it to get away from the biker guy, but then we found Lanie and everything got so crazy. I couldn't even reach Matt for two days. And when I did, he was so upset with me for partying and making an ass of myself, I couldn't get a word in. And then I got upset with him for not being more supportive. And by the time we reconciled. After my...incident?" I shrug. "It seemed like water under the bridge, so I let it go."

"I understand," Ella says. "But if we're looking for people who wanted to kill Josh Tanner, Matt would be high on the list. Do you see what I'm saying?"

I do see what she's saying, and she has a point, but I can't let on about what I know.

"Matt was with Danny all weekend," I lie. "How could he go up to the cabin and stage a suicide? In the middle of a hurricane?"

But Matt wasn't with Danny all weekend.

Danny was with my mother because Matt had to go to work.

Or so he said.

"Sure, Reagan. That makes sense. All I'm saying is, let's hope it's ruled a suicide. That would be best for all concerned. Except for my mother, that is. I think she'd like to see my father fry."

"That has to be hard, being in the middle of it," I say.

And I mean it. I don't envy Ella.

"It is, but Ted's been my rock. I don't know what I'd do without him."

We need each other, I'm starting to see. "I'm sure it was a suicide," I offer. "Remember how torn up Josh was? He even confessed to me that he loved Lanie. Right before he went for that run."

Ella shakes her head. "It's true, I'm sure. Love can make you do crazy things. And I'm thinking that kind of guilt could really push a person over the edge." She pauses as she peers at me. "And if the police question you, you'll be sure to drive that point home to them, right?"

I swallow. And then I nod. "Sure," I say. "I already did. Just like I told you."

She continues. "It's tragic, really. Don't you think? If only Lanie had taken Josh up on his offer that night, maybe none of this would have happened."

We change the subject and move on, but our unspoken pact lingers in the air. Both of us have a lot to lose if the cops start digging around into Josh's death. Both of us have everything to gain if they rule it a suicide and close the case.

So, we make small talk and carry on like we haven't a care in the world. I tell her about my new career idea. She reveals to me that she's taking over her father's business. She gives me some tips on how to handle the terrible twos. And as we say our goodbyes, I add, for good measure: "Give my best to your mother."

After all, Helen's the one who started all this—and she's the one who can drive a nail into Rob Parker's coffin and put this whole matter to rest.

FORTY-ONE
REAGAN

All afternoon, I've been on pins and needles, waiting for Matt to come home from work. Just when I thought I had a handle on my life, Ella threw me a curveball.

Matt was up at Ella's camp ten years ago.

He never told me about it.

They've kept that from me all these years.

Are there other secrets they've kept from me?

And do I want to know what they are?

There's something to be said for the idea of living in ignorant bliss. But I'm not ignorant, although I wish I was. One thing for sure is I need to explain to Matt about that kiss. It makes so much more sense to me now, though. It seemed so unlike him that he would get that upset with me about the partying. It crossed my mind that someone might have told him about the kiss. He's always been jealous of Josh, so this would just be fuel on an already simmering fire.

But who?

And why?

What would anyone have to gain?

So, I told myself that he didn't know, and I changed my mind about wanting to tell him. But all along he knew. Because he was there. And here we are, ten years later. If I hadn't tried to...if I hadn't taken all those pills, would we even be together right now? He might have never forgiven me. I feel horrible that all these years, he may have thought I was still hung up on Josh when I wasn't.

But one thing doesn't make sense. If Matt saw me kiss Josh, then why did he encourage me to go up to the camp last weekend? You would think he'd have tried to talk me out of it. A part of me thinks it might have been a test. Like maybe he asked Ella to keep an eye out and report back to him. Apparently, the two of them are close enough to keep secrets from me, and that's something he needs to answer for. Maybe deep down inside, Matt always worried that I'd settled for him over Josh. Which may have been true in the very early days, before we slept together, but couldn't be further from the truth now.

We've gotten Danny down, and we're on the sofa, about to cue up a new episode of *The Lincoln Lawyer*. And I think about that promise I made, that I'd be happy and content and wouldn't go looking for trouble. But we need to clear the air on this.

So when he points the remote and starts to press Play, I put my hand on his.

"Wait," I say. "We need to talk."

Briefly, I give him the rundown of my conversation with Ella, updating him on her father's case and giving him the context surrounding her revelation to me. "And when I asked if Ted was a suspect, and pointed out that Ted despised Josh, she threw it back in my face."

Matt's brow furrows. "Your face? How? Did you and Josh have a falling out that weekend?"

My lips press together as I take a pause, wondering how he'll interpret this. "Yeah, we did. Except that's not what she meant. Ella pointed out that if we made a list of people who had it in for Josh, you'd be high on the list."

Matt's eyes widen. "Me? Why me?"

"Because," I say. "Apparently, you were up at the camp ten years ago. And you saw me kiss him." I offer him a sympathetic head tilt, so as not to look too accusatory.

Matt blushes. "Oh shit," he says. "I had a feeling that might come out over the weekend."

"Why didn't you tell me?" I ask.

He rolls his eyes. "I don't know. With all that happened, it didn't seem important anymore. I almost lost you, Reagan. After your overdose, Ella called and told me that it meant nothing. That you were wasted. And Ella said you only kissed Josh to get away from some creepy biker guy. I shouldn't have jumped to conclusions. And then I realized I was being stupid, making such a big deal of it. And so I went to the hospital to see you, and, well, you know the rest."

"Wow. Ella did that for me?"

Funny, she didn't mention that part to me.

"Yeah," Matt says. "She did. And I asked her not to tell you I was there that night. I was worried about how it would look, like you might have thought I was stalking you or checking up on you or something."

"Oh," I say. "So, were you? Checking up on me?"

Matt's eyes widen. "No!" he says. "I went up to the camp to surprise you. Because you were mad at me for being such a tool about that weekend. And you were right. I was being a tool. I should have been there with you. Protecting you. It was one stupid weekend of fun, and you deserved to blow off some steam. It probably would have been good for me, too. And I'm sorry I let you down. If anything had happened to you that night..."

He brushes the hair back from my face and kisses me.

"It's okay," I say. "I'm fine. Nothing bad happened to me that night."

"But it could have. If I'd seen that biker guy manhandle you, I'd have..." Matt's nostrils flare as he thinks back on it, and I have to admit, it's kind of hot.

He blows out a breath. "I'd have dealt with him, that's for sure. And Josh is a douchebag for not being a friend to you that night. As far as I'm concerned, Josh Tanner got what he deserved. Blackmail? Profiting off Lanie's death? He's a creep. And I should have been with you. And I'm sorry that I wasn't."

Matt's words warm my heart, but I could not imagine my geeky husband going up against a biker. Matt's not small, mind you. He's got a solid build and he's freakishly strong. It's more how he presents. Like a guy who could do your taxes and save you a bundle of money, not a guy who could kick biker ass.

Maybe it's better he didn't see what happened with snake man. It might not have ended well for him. But it means the world to me that he had my back, unlike Josh the Blackmailer. I'm not going to lose much sleep over his death. Matt's right. Josh Tanner got what he deserved.

"I'm sorry I didn't tell you about the kiss," I say. "I was

planning on it. But when you wouldn't talk to me, I got pissed. We had that falling out, and then we made up. And with everything on our plates, it just sort of seemed beside the point."

"It's fine," he says. "We're together now."

Shaking my head, I continue. "Such a stupid misunderstanding. It could have broken us up. I guess I have Ella to thank for the fact that we're still together. Maybe I should let her know how much I appreciate it."

"She's got enough on her plate, don't you think? How about we leave the past behind. Think about the future instead. How's that for a plan?"

I smile. Matt's right, and I decide I'm not asking any questions about last weekend or where he was while my mother was watching Danny, or any of it. He's given me the perfect opening to move forward and let sleeping dogs lie.

"Speaking of the future..." I smile.

Then I start to tell him about my new career plan.

Matt nods in agreement. "I'm all for you pursuing something you're passionate about. But it's late. Could we put the details on the back burner for now? I've got better plans for this evening."

"Oh," I say. Matt loves this series. "Right. Start it up."

But I turn to him and see the steamy look in his eye. That primal hunger for me. He's not talking about the series.

Watching Matt take off his glasses and toss them aside, he transforms before my eyes.

From mild-mannered Clark Kent to Superman.

Our little secret.

Something I alluded to with Ella but that I've never come out and told anyone.

In the sack, Matt's an animal.

The first time we made love, it shocked me, but it also made Matt a lot more interesting to me. I thought he'd be bland, given the fact that he was so straightlaced and career-focused, but I was dead wrong.

I feel the power and urgency of his embrace, and I know he wants me. His bulk rubs up against me, and all thoughts of Ella and the camp and the case vanish from my mind. We whip off our clothes and he ravages my body, in the best ways possible.

When we're done, he reaches for his glasses, puts them back on, and cues up the next episode, as if it never happened. He's funny like that, the way he can go from hot to cold in the blink of an eye.

And now I'm back where I wanted to be, when I was stuck in the cabin with a potential murderer. When I was slogging through the muck. When I saw my life flash before my eyes just as that car sent me flying into the air.

Back where I belong.

With my husband and son.

And nothing will ever come between me and my family again.

EPILOGUE

ONE YEAR LATER

It's a week before finals and I've been cramming for my exams. Anatomy and Physiology II, Microbiology, and Medical Terminology, the last of my prerequisites for the nursing program. It's been a busy year, but a productive one. I've been volunteering at a local hospital and I'm confident that this new career path will be a good fit for me. It's very busy, which suits me.

I've come a long way. No more moping around the house. Danny started preschool and he seems to love it. Matt and I are going strong. I'm in a good place, making new friends with some of the preschool moms, and I hope that continues.

Because I've got big news to share. Yep. We're expecting. A girl this time, we're pretty sure. Blood test results aren't always accurate, but most of the time they are. We'll soon be the four of us, fingers crossed, if nothing goes wrong. But there's an uneasiness settling in the pit of my stomach. Maybe it's morning sickness. I didn't get that with Danny, but every pregnancy is different. I'm almost through my third month, so I'm not sure why it would start now. Maybe I'm pushing myself too hard.

I need to take a break, so I close the books, flip on the TV, and search for my guilty pleasure: true crime shows. Matt thumbs his nose at these shows, and he thinks I'm nuts for watching them. He even suggested that they contribute to my anxiety. But I think it's the opposite. Shows like these make me realize that I don't have it so bad. The cold cases are so sad. I can't imagine never knowing what happened to a loved one. It must be agonizing.

Speaking of cold cases, Ella's father was never indicted for Josh Tanner's murder. He took a plea deal for Lanie Martin's homicide, and he's serving ten years for voluntary manslaughter, although everyone expects he'll get out sooner. His attorney couldn't sell the involuntary charge, since he admitted to the altercation where he grabbed her and she ran from him. But he still swears he never meant to kill her.

Josh's manner of death has been ruled "undetermined," which means they don't know if it was a suicide or a homicide. It also means the police could file charges at any time if any more evidence comes to light, and there's no statute of limitations on murder. Technically, Josh's death is now a cold case. I imagine Ella and I will both be holding our collective breaths for the foreseeable future. We never did find out what was said in that suicide note. And if there's no trial, I bet we never will.

Although I've hardly been able to admit this to myself, I checked up a little on my husband. Took a peek at Matt's credit card receipts for the weekend of Josh's death, just for my own peace of mind, to see if there was anything incriminating. The only red flag was that he got gas twice, which seems like a lot of gas for one weekend. But then he could have been driving around a lot, looking at property damage. I'm not taking it any further, though. I'm carrying our baby. I don't need the additional stress.

Searching through the episodes of cold cases featured on a lesser-known streaming series I like, I land on a title that stops me in my tracks:

Vanished in the High Peaks.

Scrolling past it would probably be the right thing to do. It's a little close to home, after all.

But of course, I don't.

Instead, I click on it.

The story of Bobby Wilks begins.

Most of these missing persons cases are not like the ones you see splashed all over the news. Beautiful women. Darling young children. Those are the ones that make the headlines. But the vast majority are not like that, and beyond the immediate family, nobody seems to give a damn about any of them.

Drug addicts and criminals. Prostitutes and troubled teens. The kind of people who the police or even the victim's own relatives and friends assume left of their own accord, or met some fate they were destined for, given their track records. Or simply average-looking people who don't happen to be glitzy or click-worthy enough for a page one story.

Bobby Wilks was one of those people, and the only person who seems to care at all is his older sister Sharon, a bleached blonde who looks to be around fifty. She has craggy, weathered skin and dark crimson lipstick that bleeds into the smoking lines that frame her mouth.

He was a cute little kid, she says.

They always are.

Some pictures flash of a little towhead guy, around six or so, with missing front teeth and an elfin grin. But then it all goes bad. Bobby and Sharon had a tough childhood, she discloses. Dad ran off, Mom was working or drinking or out with some random guy. Sis tried her best to keep little Bobby on the straight and narrow.

But, needing a father figure, Bobby joined a local biker gang and dropped out of high school. And by the time he disappeared, he had the kind of rap sheet that made him hard to care about as a missing person, or even a dead body.

Drug possession. Assault and battery charges. Sexual assault as a minor, which Sharon swears was a trumped-up charge by a jilted girlfriend.

And so, when Bobby Wilks went missing eleven years ago, nobody tried too hard to find him. And when they discovered his skeletal remains deep in the woods of the High Peaks region nine months ago, tucked away in a gully about half a mile from the path I stumbled onto when I was fleeing from Ella's camp, Sharon finally got the closure she was looking for.

Dental records confirmed that it was him. His most recent photo flashes on the TV screen. It's a photo of a guy in his thirties, beer can in hand, smiling for the camera—with a tattoo of a snake wrapped around a cross covering his forearm.

My heart nearly skips a beat.

It's him.

The biker guy.

So far, the police and the medical examiner don't think foul play was involved, although the sister seems to believe otherwise. His skull was cracked, ostensibly by a rock, but it could have been from the fall, based on where they found him. He probably stumbled and died of exposure, they told her.

Sharon's not buying it. He had beef with a biker from another gang around that time, the sister reveals, and she thinks he may have been murdered. She appeals to the public for information, and then they're out. As the credits roll, they disclose that Sharon died of a heart attack, about a month after they filmed the episode. Unlucky family, it seems.

Two suspicious deaths.

Both in the woods surrounding Ella's camp.

Matt was up there at the camp that night of Lanie's death.

The night that Billy Wilks accosted me.

Could Matt have…?

I picture the way my husband transforms before my eyes when we make love, all that hot passion he keeps stored up inside, and I realize that passion can cut both ways. And if Ella gets wind of this cold case, will she suspect something? Would she think that if Matt did this, that he might have murdered Josh and tried to frame him for Lanie's murder?

It won't look good if this all comes out. But then, she didn't even see the guy. She won't know it was the same person. I mentioned a tattoo, but I didn't describe it. Good thing I never told the police about him.

His story hasn't gotten a lot of press, and from what I've

seen of these kinds of cases, it probably won't, especially with his sister out of the picture. But I'll never forget it, and I wish I hadn't clicked on the episode.

Was it fate?

Did someone want me to know this?

A memory flashes before my eyes, and suddenly, the last piece of the puzzle snaps into place. My stomach sinks as it plays out in my head like a movie, strikingly vivid. My memories are still somewhat out of order, but I'm certain this happened after Josh and Lanie insulted me but before I went over to Brady. I walked into the woods to pee.

I'm there.

In the woods.

Alone.

As I'm zipping up my pants, someone grabs me from behind and spins me around.

"There you are," he says. "We've got some unfinished business."

It's him.

Snake man.

He latches onto my arm and I scream out loud. He's so strong.

I swing my foot up to try and kick him in the balls, but I miss.

This amuses him. "I told you I like 'em feisty. Keep it up."

When he pushes me to the ground to subdue me, he stumbles and falls onto his side. He's pretty drunk, but so am I.

I grab a rock.

A grisly cracking sound fills my ears.

I get up and run.

And that's all I remember.

There's no connection between this memory and my dancing at the firepit.

There's no memory of me dragging him to where the body was found.

And how would I have ever been able to do that?

The answer is, I couldn't have.

Maybe my mind is playing tricks on me again. I like this idea. I just saw this episode, and I'm inserting snake man into my dream or memory or whatever that was.

But I know it's not true. I'm sure this happened. It's real, much more real than the vague one with Rob Parker's face, which I'm sure now never actually happened. The vision I saw wasn't about Lanie's death. It was about me, and the fact that I was assaulted—and that I fought back. It was my scream I heard in the woods, reverberating in my subconscious. My mind must have blocked it out to protect me.

Did I kill him?

And Matt was there that night.

Matt could have seen what he did to me and finished what I started. Maybe that's why it took him so long to come see me, and why I couldn't reach him for two days. Is that what Matt meant when he said he had my back in ways I didn't know?

I stare into space for a good long while, trying to wrap my head around this, wishing I could remember more than what I saw, but also wishing I'd never watched that episode.

But I know what I need to do.

Picking up the phone, I make a call.

"Reagan," Ella says. "What a lovely surprise. I was just thinking about you. We've got something this weekend, but next weekend is good for a double date. I'm sorry I didn't get back to you sooner."

"It's fine," I say.

We catch each other up, although there's not much to report. We promised to stay close this time. And we have, bonded by our mutual interests and concerns. Ted and Matt seem to have bonded, too. They've started playing tennis together.

And then I get to the point of the call.

"Ella, I actually called to tell you something," I say.

"Sure, what is it?"

"Well, it's good news, actually," I tell her. "I'm pregnant, but keep that on the down-low. We're not telling everyone just yet."

"Congratulations!" she cries out.

I continue. "And we'd like you and Ted to be the godparents for our baby girl."

"Oh, that's just fantastic," Ella exclaims. "We'd be honored," she gushes. "You're like a sister to me. The sister I never had. I'm so glad we've grown close again, Reagan. I hope it stays like this forever this time."

"Me too, Ella," I say.

You have no idea.

A BATCH of oatmeal chocolate chip cookies, Matt's favorite, sits on our coffee table, cooling off, while I struggle to make sense of this new information. We got through dinner and I feigned normalcy. Matt went upstairs to take a shower, so I'm watching the video a second time. I pause the video on the face of my assailant, trying to see if I missed something or if it might trigger my mind to remember more from that night. Anything that could fill in some of the blanks.

Matt thunders into the living room, catching me by surprise. "Reagan, Ted called to tell me..."

I thought he was taking a shower.

Fumbling for the remote, I try to get the image off the TV screen. The image of Bobby Wilks, smiling for the camera, with a beer can in his hand, but I'm too slow.

Matt stops in his tracks and he lets out a sigh. "You and your true crime," he says, shaking his head. "I told you not to watch those shows, Reagan."

We lock eyes. "That's the guy," I say. "The one who accosted me at the camp."

But from the look on Matt's face, I didn't need to tell him.

"I know," he says.

"You were there," I say.

Matt nods.

My stomach lurches, and I feel the hairs on the back of my neck stand up.

Why didn't he tell me about this?

What does this mean?

Matt sits down next to me with a look of concern on his face. He puts a hand on my forearm. "How much do you remember?" he asks me.

I shrug. "Bobby Wilks attacked me. I fell to the ground. I grabbed a rock. I heard a cracking sound. And then I got up and ran."

Looking off into the distance, I picture the night in my

mind's eye, trying to remember if I saw Matt there. But I don't think I did. "And what about you? Or do I even want to know?"

"Reagan, do you trust me?" my husband asks.

I swallow, but my hesitation speaks volumes.

"It's not a difficult question to answer, Reagan. And if you don't trust me, then what is all this for?" He waves his hands around our living room, a picture of domestic bliss, the scent of freshly baked cookies and melting chocolate wafting over toward us.

I think hard about all that's at stake before I answer.

"It's hard to trust you when I find out you were up at the camp ten years ago. When I find out you and Ella have been keeping things from me. And when I find out that you knew that this biker guy attacked me and you kept it to yourself. Tell me what's going on, Matt. I can handle anything. Anything except more lies."

Matt stands now and starts to pace around the room, running his hand through his hair. "It's not that simple, Reagan. We have two kids to think about."

"What's that supposed to mean?"

"It means if we both know the truth, then we're both vulnerable. But there are a few things I can tell you that might make you feel better, at least about me. About us. Would that help?"

"I guess?"

"First, I'll give you a hypothetical. Do you know much about the self-defense doctrine?"

I shrug. "I guess? Not a lot. But I know the basics. If you kill someone in self-defense, it's not a crime."

"Well, it's not quite that simple. The amount of force has

to be in proportion to the threat, and you can only use the least amount of force to subdue the person. And if you have a chance to escape and you don't take it, well, that also complicates things."

"Are you saying that one of us…"

"I'm not saying anything about you or me. This is purely hypothetical," he offers.

But I'm not having it. I throw up my hands. "Matt? No! That's not enough. Are you talking about you? Or are you talking about me? I need to know."

He sighs. "I told you I'd do anything to protect you. And I meant it. You went running back to the house after you got away from him, but he started after you. You didn't see me. I came at the tail end and saw what was happening. And let's just say he didn't get very far."

Wow.

I sit with this for a few minutes.

Then I say, "And what's the second thing?"

"Ted and I have kept in touch over the years," he says. "We had a common enemy, if you get my drift. Josh knew Lanie was pregnant with Rob Parker's child. And he saw things that night, too. Things that you did. Things that Ted and I did. And he used that to his monetary advantage. It needed to stop."

I take a deep breath as it sinks in; what this means.

Did Ted help Matt move the body?

Was Josh blackmailing us, too?

But there's really only one thing I need to know.

"Okay. Now it's my turn. I'm going to ask you one question," I say. "And I'm going to need the truth. Were you up at the cabin, the weekend of the reunion?"

This is something I need to know. I can handle it if Matt finished what I started with snake man. I can handle it if he covered up what we did and dragged his body deep into the woods. And I understand why he kept it all from me to protect me. But I couldn't live with a cold-blooded murderer who killed Josh and tried to make it look like a suicide.

"No," he says, without hesitation. "I wasn't there that weekend. I was working. You can check with the adjustor. He was with me the whole time. Because I didn't need to be. I had a hunch the problem would take care of itself. That was the plan. They would have this reunion, and the Parkers would confront Josh and put a stop to it. At least, that's what they told me. They didn't say they were going to murder him. But then, they wouldn't, would they?"

"Do you know what happened to Josh?" I ask.

"I do not," he says. "But it looks like they're getting closer to the truth. Ted called five minutes ago. That's what I was coming to tell you. There's been a break in the case."

"A break?"

"Yeah. Apparently, Helen Parker found an old computer that belonged to her husband in the attic, along with Josh's handwritten ransom notes. And when they dove into the search history, they found evidence that Rob Parker bought a ghost gun on the dark web. It's not a slam dunk, but it doesn't look good for Ella's father. He might end up in prison for a lot longer than ten years."

"Wow," I say. "I didn't see that coming. Do you think he did it? Killed Josh and tried to stage it as a suicide? Did they find out what the note said?"

"Yeah. It was short. *Sorry, Lanie.* Or something like that. Pretty vague."

"Seems like if Rob Parker was planning to frame Josh and make it look like a suicide, he'd have written a better note. Maybe Josh really did kill himself," I offer. "Maybe the thought of being exposed as a blackmailer and a fraud was too much for him."

"Or someone's trying to frame Rob Parker," Matt adds.

My head tilts to the side as I consider this. "Helen found the computer. Do you think she was angry enough to set her husband up? Maybe Josh killed himself, but Helen figured she could frame her husband to get back at him. Or do you think maybe they were all in on it together, and Rob Parker's taking the fall?"

"I think that's not our problem; that's what I think. But seeing as how you made Ted and Ella the godparents to our unborn child, I suppose we're in this thing with them for the long haul. Can we move on now?" Matt asks.

"We can," I say. "But I think we were stuck with them, anyway. Ted and Ella know what we did. We need to keep them close."

"Ella doesn't know. Only Ted. He never told her, as far as I know. For the same reasons I didn't tell you. You're probably right, though, about keeping them close," Matt says. "But what's say we put them on the back burner for tonight. Danny's asleep. Let's enjoy the evening."

"Sounds good to me," I say.

Matt reaches for a cookie and takes a bite.

I'm in awe of the way he can compartmentalize and move on. But there's one thing I remember that Matt hasn't commented on, and I think it's gallant, how he's trying to protect me, so I don't disclose to him one last detail about my recovered memory. Maybe Matt finished him off, but I was no damsel in distress. I slammed that rock against Bobby Wilks' skull—twice. Maybe I killed him. Maybe I didn't. But I did some damage, and I'd do it again.

In a heartbeat.

"What do you want to watch tonight?" he asks.

"You pick this time," I say.

Matt scrolls through the offerings while I check my phone.

He lands on a movie. A classic.

Matt looks over at me with a smirk on his face and shrugs.

My husband's sure got a dark sense of humor.

I smile and nod my approval:

Murder on the Orient Express.

ACKNOWLEDGMENTS

My sincere thanks to the many people who helped me craft this novel and bring it to completion. Thanks goes out once again to my husband who brainstormed with me endlessly when I hit plot challenges and who also read countless drafts of my manuscript.

Thanks to my invaluable alpha and beta readers Robin, Susan, and Donna who offered excellent suggestions and encouragement. Thanks to my chief beta reader Christina Yother whose suggestions and attention to detail went way beyond a typical beta read, offering valuable ideas to make the manuscript better. Thanks to my fabulous editor at BooksGoSocial, and to the entire team for their expert advice in marketing and promotions.

Thanks to all of my advance copy readers on Booksprout and NetGalley who take the time to read my books and post their reviews. Thanks to fellow thriller authors R.G. Belsky, Douglas Corleone, Tracey Devlyn, Laurie Dove, Noelle W. Ihli, Leslie Lutz, and Neil Turner for their beta reads, blurbs, support, encouragement and camaraderie. Please check out their fabulous thrillers.

Finally, thanks so much to my readers. You are why I keep writing, and I am so grateful for the time you take to read my books as well as rate and comment on them. I read all of my reviews and it helps me to improve, so please keep them coming. I really appreciate it. For updates, book reviews and special offers, please go to www.bonnietraymore.com and sign up for my quarterly newsletter.

ABOUT THE AUTHOR

Bonnie Traymore is the award-winning, Amazon charts bestselling author of eight domestic suspense thrillers. Her books feature strong but relatable female protagonists who find themselves in extraordinary circumstances. Originally from the New York City area, she's lived in Honolulu with her family for the last few decades.

THE BLUFF: A THRILLER
PLEASE ENJOY A SAMPLE

PROLOGUE

Doug Mitchell takes in the shoreline of Lake Michigan, letting his Sundancer drift around in the currents. The sight of his house high atop the bluff reminds him of what is at stake. The vote is tonight, and it's sure to be one hell of an evening. A cool wind whips up what little sand remains on the shrinking beach, and he can see the bare patch of earth where the southern stairs collapsed two years ago. But he feels safe and warm on the deck, with the soon-to-be-setting sun still overhead, beaming down on him.

It's not the same shoreline it was decades ago, but then the world is an ever-changing place. He knows this, although he doesn't let on about it to most people. Right now, his mind is drifting to another place, and he feels a delightful stirring. He pictures the curve of her back. Her slender, graceful neck. The look on her face when he makes her moan. He takes another sip of his cocktail, closes his eyes, and sinks into it.

After a few minutes, a different kind of feeling washes

over him. He's dizzy. And tired. Way too tired. He's barely had one drink. He opens his eyes, and the world appears blurry. He feels clumsy. Almost immobile. Shaking his head, he tries to snap out of it, but everything's...

Fuzzy.

Confused.

Off.

He came out here alone, he thinks, although he didn't check the cabin before leaving the dock. A figure is standing on the deck now, too far away from him to make out who it is. It's someone, though, and even with his mind dulled, he knows this is not good.

Seized with panic, he struggles to pull himself out of the quagmire. Finding a last burst of strength, he attempts to spring up and go on the offensive, but his legs are like rubber. His body rocks forward a bit, accomplishing nothing.

He sinks back into oblivion as the figure approaches.

You?

ONE

KATE

I arrive five minutes late for my meeting, breathless from my run in from the parking lot. The proceedings haven't started yet. Rushing in, I whip off my scarf and coat and take a seat.

Just in time.

The stage is set for a contentious evening. Tonight, the town council will vote on the pressing issue of the crumbling bluff. I head up the shoreline committee, and I've been invited here this evening to present my plan, one of two the board will consider.

"Hi, Kate," the board member next to me says. "Glad you made it."

She gives my shoulder a squeeze, confirming that I've got her vote.

"Of course," I say. "Sorry, I'm late."

A tingling sensation creeps up my spine, and a feeling of dread squeezes my stomach like a vise. Perhaps it's the weather. It's early fall, but it may as well be the dead of winter. It's bitter cold and gray, with intermittent downpours. Sheets of water batter my home at night, threatening to sweep it into the lake, and the howling wind whipping off Lake Michigan has been keeping me up. It's the same weather we were having when my husband met his untimely death a year ago, which is likely stirring up some buried feelings. A widow at forty-one. Not the way I expected my life to go when I moved here six years ago.

"The meeting of the Crest Lake Township board of directors is now in session," the president proclaims, banging his gavel with the countenance of a man desperate for power and relevance. Sam Bolger's his name.

Sam takes role, and it's lost on nobody that Doug Mitchell is absent. I fiddle with a strand of hair, twirling it between my fingers. It looks darker in this light, almost auburn. My eyes search the room, and hushed tones fill the silence as people whisper to each other.

Where the hell is Doug?

Are we really going to start without him?

I hope he's okay.

His allies look concerned, naturally, but even his opponents seem troubled, although that could be an act. It would be unacceptable to show their glee in the event they were feeling it. But I'm not feeling smug or excited or victorious. I'm feeling nervous. Doug is scheduled to present the opposing plan, and there's no way he would intentionally miss this meeting. His absence magnifies the gnawing feeling inside me that something is about to go terribly wrong.

Tempers have been flaring over what to do about the eroding bluff. The police had to be called during the last public hearing. There have even been a few death threats, anonymous posts and phone messages that most of us brushed off.

Silly, really. We're all on the same team, trying to fight Mother Nature. Desperate to give ourselves the illusion of control. Struggling to keep our large, lakefront luxury homes from plummeting onto the shrinking shoreline that hugs the massive body of water eighty feet below the fragile bluff.

On some level, we all know that whatever we do will only be a stop-gap in the big picture of geological time, and I can't help but wonder if that's what's making people so angry. Humanity's stubborn insistence that we can bend the planet to our will. It's obvious that we can't, and perhaps it's easier to blame each other than to face the realization that humans are at the mercy of forces we don't really understand and can no longer control.

The president seems to be stalling, fumbling with his computer as he tries to pull up the agenda and project it onto the TV screen. The board member to my right shares a theory with me. Perhaps Doug's pulling a stunt for dramatic effect, she whispers in my ear. Maybe the president's in on it —he's on Doug's side—and Doug will come bursting in at the last minute, waving some new study in his hands. After a few moments, it's clear to everyone that that's not going to happen.

Sam tables the vote for the time being and moves on to other issues. The board gets to work. There are a handful of mundane items on the agenda aside from the one that matters to me—what to do about the shoreline. I wait patiently as the board members work through other business, waiting for Doug's arrival, my palms starting to sweat. He's a board member, but I'm not.

I wonder what will happen if he doesn't show up. Will they postpone the vote, or will it go my way by default, with my proposal the only option? Item after item is addressed, and I can feel my pulse starting to race as they tick them off.

Parcel tax proposal.

New library budget.

Changes to the vacation rental rules.

My stomach is in knots now. If the vote goes my way, it will be a Pyrrhic victory, inflicting massive economic consequences on my lakefront neighbors. Doug's plan to simply shore up the bluff at the toe, the spot where the waves hit and wear it down, is the simple one. The less expensive one. It's got the environmental groups up in arms, though. They've grown increasingly vocal over the last few years.

The environmentalists want to force the removal of all existing seawalls, like the one Doug Mitchell installed in front of his home, and ban all such structures. Let nature take its course. Force lakefront owners to move back their homes or demolish them if they are in danger of falling off the bluff. But none of them are on the shoreline committee, and none are on the board. They'll be upset whichever way it goes tonight.

My plan is a compromise of sorts. If I win, there will be consequences. Expensive ones that will dramatically reduce some people's property values and limit beach access for everyone. And lots of visceral anger, much of it directed at me, especially from my wealthy lakefront neighbors, who will absorb most of the cost. Several million dollars, split between ten of us. Sweat beads form at my temples as the minutes tick along to the rhythm of the cheap wall clock mounted above my seat.

ONE

Why do they keep it so hot in here?

The council meets at the town center, a small, institutional structure that used to serve as a middle school. The chairs are small and uncomfortable. I sit up and twist from side to side, trying to stop my lower back from cramping up. After an hour or so, there's nothing left on the agenda but the bluff, and I'm wondering if they'll postpone my presentation and the vote.

A knock at the door startles us.

Police, a voice calls out.

The door opens, and a young officer enters tentatively, crouching his way into the room. It's a tight community, and he's likely a bit intimidated. We're a powerful bunch. If he ran into one of us around town, I imagine he'd be deferential. But this isn't a coffee shop or a grocery store, and this isn't a social call.

After a moment, he straightens up, and his face registers the requisite look of authority. "Doug Mitchell's been reported missing," he says. "He went out on his boat earlier today and never returned. The Coast Guard is conducting a search."

My stomach sinks. I'm sure I've turned a shade paler. Gasps echo around the room. We all sit with the shocking news for a few moments as the officer bites his lower lip.

He continues. "We're going to need to interview all of you. Detective Whittaker is on his way. Please stay seated and be patient."

With that, the vote is delayed.

ONE

Travis Whittaker leans back in his chair, eyeing me. I can see tension lines on the detective's forehead. He seems to have aged since I last saw him, although his thick, dark head of hair reveals few strands of gray. It's his eyes. They look heavy and full, like the weight of the world sits behind them.

He's been working his way through the group, and I'm second-to-last. It would have been better to get it over with. Waiting around only increased the tension. Nobody knew what to say to each other, so nothing but awkward silence filled the space between us as we stood in the hallway, waiting for our turns to go in and be interviewed.

"So, Ms. Breslow. You arrived five minutes late," he says.

"I just said that," I reply, immediately regretting my sharp tone.

The detective's nostrils flare ever so slightly. He's an attractive man for his age—early fifties—with a neatly trimmed beard and dark, steely eyes. Right now, though, he looks menacing.

"Yes. I was about five minutes late," I say in a softer tone. My throat feels as if it's about to close up on me.

He narrows his eyes on me, and I look away. I catch myself absent-mindedly stroking my neck and stop myself, placing my hands on the tabletop.

This feels all too familiar.

"And why were you late?"

"The rain," I offer. "It got heavy when I was driving down Lakeside." Tapping my fingers on the tabletop, I search for something to add. "I had to drive more slowly."

He nods and jots something down on his notepad. Almost everyone at the meeting had to drive down that road in the rain. It's not a very good excuse, but it's all I can give him.

"Did Doug Mitchell give you any indication that he was planning to miss the meeting tonight?" he asks.

"No, not at all," I reply. "We were all shocked when he didn't show up tonight."

"Have you heard from him today?" he says.

I shake my head no.

"When's the last time you had any contact with him?" he asks.

I look off to the side, struggling to keep myself focused and calm. I turn back to him. "In person?"

"In general," Whittaker replies.

"We've been on the same email and text chain over the last week or so. Exchanging information in anticipation of the vote."

"You didn't answer my question."

I swallow. He's already seen our text stream, I assume. "Yesterday. Around seven in the evening."

"Was that an email or a text?"

"It was a text."

"What did it say?"

I pull up my phone, hold it in my palm, and let him read the exchange. His eyes rest on my last line to Doug Mitchell.

> If you do that, I'll bury you.

It would have been less stressful for me if Whittaker's face had registered some kind of surprise. Instead, he closes his notepad and puts his pen down. I struggle to keep a neutral look on my face. Then he informs me that I can leave and asks me to send in the next board member.

I start for the door, but then turn back to him. "In paperwork," I offer. "I meant I'd bury him in paperwork." Then I turn away again and continue to the door.

"Don't leave town," he calls out. "We're sure to have more questions as the investigation develops."

I nod and keep walking.

As my car winds up the dark, curvy, tree-lined road to my lakefront home, I struggle to steady my shaking hands. This night already had me on edge, and I can feel my pulse racing as I reach the bend in the road near the top. The part where the drop-off is the steepest. They replaced the guardrail with another one that looks exactly the same as the last one, which proved to be inadequate.

What was the point of that?

Sometimes, I can ignore it and drive right past. On sunny days, when the sky is bright and the birds chirp and all is well in the universe. It looks so different in the daylight. But tonight is foggy and foreboding, and I drive slowly. So slowly, I'd probably get a ticket if an officer was behind me. I don't look to my right, though, because then I have to picture it. And imagine the look of terror on my husband's face as he plunged through the rail and over the side.

What was he thinking?
Or was he not thinking at all?
Did he scream?
Or was there no time?

A chill runs up my spine as I turn carefully around the bend and breathe a sigh of relief. Sometimes, I get the sensation that he's in the car with me, and I can almost feel his breath on my neck.

Now, Doug is missing, and I have no idea what to do next or what this means for me and my shoreline plan. All I know is I have to sell my house and get out of this town before I lose my mind.

Or worse.

If you like this sample, please check my website at www.bonnietraymore.com for current retail availability.

Made in United States
Troutdale, OR
07/06/2025